'You know you

'Yes.' How could she

'But?' He lifted one dark eyebrow in sardonic question.

'I'm. . .not going to go to bed with you,' Shelley forced out, struggling to sound convincing. 'I'm. . .married.'

He laughed in stinging mockery. 'Dammit, I know you're married,' Saul grated. 'But you're not in love with him—you were never in love with him.' It was a statement, not a question. 'You couldn't have kissed me like that if you were.'

'That's not the point,' she responded evasively. 'He's. . .my husband.' She finally managed to lift her eyes to meet his. 'I can't just pretend that he doesn't exist.'

He drew in a long, deep breath, as if struggling to maintain his own self-control. 'All right,' he conceded, finally letting her go. 'If that's the way it has to be. It seems a little. . .ironic that you should have such high principles, when he appears to have none at all.'

Susanne McCarthy grew up in south London but she always wanted to live in the country, and shortly after her marriage she moved to Shropshire with her husband. They live in a house on a hill with lots of dogs and cats. She loves to travel—but she loves to come home. As well as her writing, she still enjoys her career as a teacher in adult education, though she only works part-time now.

Recent titles by the same author:

BAD INFLUENCE
HER PERSONAL BODYGUARD

A MARRIED WOMAN?

BY
SUSANNE McCARTHY

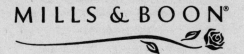

MILLS & BOON®

First published in Great Britain 1997
Harlequin Mills & Boon Limited,
Eton House, 18-24 Paradise Road, Richmond, Surrey TW9 1SR

© Susanne McCarthy 1997

ISBN 0 263 80148 9

Set in Times 10 on 11½ pt. by
Rowland Phototypesetting Limited
Bury St Edmunds, Suffolk

01-9706-50195-D

Printed and bound in Great Britain
by Mackays of Chatham PLC, Chatham

CHAPTER ONE

'AND I'll huff, and I'll puff, and I'll *blow* your house down. . . Ah, there's Daddy at last.' Shelley lifted her head from her small daughter's story book as the doorbell rang. 'He must have forgotten his key.'

Emma, tucked up in her cot with Fred Bear by her side, gurgled contentedly. The tooth she had been cutting was safely through, almost completing the top set and, hopefully, giving her a respite for a while from the discomfort that had made her uncharacteristically grizzly for the past few days.

Shelley lifted the cot side and clicked it securely into place before hurrying downstairs to open the door, a small frown creasing her smooth forehead. It was most unlike Colin to be late home, or to mislay his key; in the seven weeks they had been married, she had found that she could virtually set her watch by him.

But then that was what she had wanted, she reminded herself quickly, tucking a long, wayward strand of russet hair back behind her ears: someone reliable. She could no longer afford to think only of herself—she had Emma to watch out for. Crazy idiots who got themselves killed in motorbike accidents were not the best father material—however doting.

'Coming!' she called as the bell rang again, impatiently. That was unlike Colin too, she reflected as she crossed the hall and opened the inner porch door— he was the most placid, even-tempered man she had ever met.

But it wasn't Colin's silhouette outlined against the bubble-glass of the front door by the light of the street-lamp across the road; this was someone several inches taller, and rather broader in the shoulder. For a moment she hesitated, and then slid on the chain, silently thanking Colin for his insistence on that basic piece of security equipment—she had never bothered to use it before, dismissing it as an unnecessary nuisance.

'Mrs Clarke?'

Her heart kicked sharply against her ribs. She knew that deep, slightly husky voice, and, peering warily around the door, she instantly recognised the hard-boned, hawkish profile. Saul Rainer—Colin's boss.

She had met him only once, just two weeks after she and Colin had got married. It had been the tenth anniversary of his takeover of the company, and he had hired one of London's top nightclubs for the evening, inviting all his senior staff to the celebration. She had danced with him—just the one dance, and only because it was expected of her; he had danced with all the wives. It had been a brief, formal encounter that he had probably forgotten in minutes—but she hadn't, hard as she had tried.

So what was he doing here now, standing on her door-step, the collar of his coat turned up against the drizzling rain?

'May I come in, Mrs Clarke?' It was a voice that was accustomed to being obeyed.

She hesitated; with Colin not at home, she would have preferred not to let him in. But this was Saul Rainer, after all—head of one of the Britain's most successful private companies; she could hardly leave him out there getting wet. So reluctantly she slipped off the chain and

opened the door, instinctively drawing back—
retreating—as he stepped into the narrow hall.

His presence seemed to dominate the space around
him. It was more than just his height, though he was
certainly tall—even she had to look up at him, which
for her, at five feet ten in her stockinged feet, was quite
unusual. No, it was something in that air of cool self-
possession that almost bordered on arrogance, in that
indefinable aura of male power that she would have
preferred to be able to deny.

She would have preferred to be able to deny the bitter-
sweet tug of forbidden attraction she felt too, but she
was too honest with herself to pretend that it wasn't still
there, perhaps even more powerful than on that night she
had first met him.

He wasn't exactly classically handsome, but there was
something. . .arresting about his features. His hair was
straight and very dark, brushed crisply back from a high,
intelligent forehead. His eyes were dark too, glinting
from beneath straight black brows—eyes that seemed to
see right through you. His nose was strongly aquiline,
and there were deep, slashing lines on each side of his
mouth—a mouth that was firmly drawn and apparently
unused to smiling.

He glanced around the shadowed hall, the grim
expression he wore causing her a sudden stab of alarm.
'Is there. . .something wrong?' she asked a little belatedly. 'Has something happened to Colin?'

'I was hoping you could answer that question for me,
Mrs Clarke,' he responded, his voice hard. 'Do you know
where your husband is?'

'No.' She shook her head, puzzled. 'He usually gets
home from work by about seven.' A glance at her watch
told her that it was nearly eight o'clock.

'He hasn't been at work today—nor did he ring in to say he was sick.'

'He wasn't sick,' she returned, even more bemused. 'At least. . .I know he's been working very hard lately.' She slanted him an accusing glare. 'Ever since the chief accountant went into hospital he's been trying to do his job as well as his own—he's been bringing work home every single night, and sometimes sitting up till midnight to get it done.'

He lifted one dark eyebrow in sardonic enquiry. 'Is that so? He never told me he was having any difficulty coping.'

Something in the tone of his voice made her look up at him in puzzled enquiry. 'What do you mean by that?'

He appeared to hesitate for a fraction of a second before responding. 'There's some money missing from one of the accounts. Rather a lot of money, as a matter of fact. Of course it could be just a mistake—as you say, he *has* been working very hard. . .' But the unmistakable implication was that he seriously doubted that explanation.

But Colin, steal money from his employer? The idea was ludicrous! Her green eyes flashed him a look of fine indignation. 'You surely don't think—?' A loud wail of protest from upstairs interrupted her. 'Oh, excuse me. . . Look, you'd better go into the sitting room for a minute.' She opened the door, aware that it was rather cold in there—but she'd be damned if she'd bother to put the fire on for him. 'Make yourself comfortable,' she invited, coolly polite. 'I'll just settle Emma and then I'll be back.'

She left him and hurried up the stairs, grateful for the moment's respite. She really shouldn't let herself be so. . .disturbed by him, she scolded herself sensibly— after all, he was only a man. And she was a married woman, with a small child. But it was something she just couldn't control.

The nursery was on the second floor of the tall old house. She still remembered so well how she and Luke had decorated it with such excitement and anticipation two years ago, the big biker in his studded leather jacket frowning over a choice of rabbit or teddy-bear wallpaper as the sales-girl had stood apprehensively by. They had chosen the teddy-bears.

Emma was standing up in her cot, her cries transformed to a huge, rosy-cheeked smile as Shelley appeared. Luke hadn't lived to see his daughter growing up, she reflected, still with a trace of bitterness; she had been just six weeks old when some idiot in a hurry had pulled out of a junction and sent the vulnerable motorbike and its rider catapulting across the busy dual carriageway—'*I'm sorry—I didn't see him.*'

She had lived with that aching well of loneliness for almost eighteen months before she had met Colin. It hadn't exactly been love at first sight, but he had been kind, and amusing, and he had been good with Emma. She had been rather surprised when he had asked her to marry him so soon after they had met—even he had laughingly admitted that he had never expected himself to be the sort to go in for a whirlwind romance.

To be honest, she hadn't been very sure at the time that it was a good idea; she had even warned him that she didn't know if she could ever feel the same about him as she had about Luke. But he had persuaded her that it didn't matter, that they could build a successful marriage on friendship, on mature considerations like mutual trust and respect. And so just six weeks after he had helped her off the bus with Emma's pushchair, they had stood on the steps of the local register office as husband and wife.

They had slipped very quickly into a nice, safe routine—a routine that had been abruptly shattered tonight, with Colin over an hour late home, and his boss sitting downstairs on the mulberry-coloured sofa in the front room, hinting at all sorts of dubious goings-on that couldn't have anything to do with her prosaic, predictable husband.

She scooped Emma up out of her cot. The toddler would take a while to settle, and she couldn't just leave Saul Rainer downstairs on his own. 'All right, chick, you get to stay up late,' she murmured, dropping a kiss on her daughter's soft blonde curls. 'Let's go downstairs and see what the horrid man has to say about your Daddy-Colin.'

As she turned, she caught a glimpse of her reflection in the mirrored door of the wardrobe. Saul Rainer could be forgiven for wondering what on earth his respectable assistant chief accountant was doing married to someone so. . .oddball, she mused with a touch of dry humour.

At the office do, for Colin's sake, she had dressed in a fairly conventional style, in a flower-sprigged dress she had made herself, and her simplest earrings, her wild hair tamed into a neat coil at the back of her head. But this evening she was wearing her customary black—she had worn little else since she had been a rebellious seventeen-year-old trying to make some sort of statement against the boring suburban values that her stepmother had been intent on imposing on her—and had on a black roll-neck sweater, short black skirt and opaque black tights, set off by jangling silver earrings that almost swept her shoulders. Her russet hair was drawn up into a loose knot on top of her head, falling in a tangle of pre-Raphaelite curls halfway down her back, and her nails were varnished a fascinating shade of purple.

The face that looked back at her from over the child's golden head was delicately boned, the skin creamy fair. Kitten, Luke used to call her, for her slanting green eyes. . . But Luke was gone now, she reminded herself crisply—and she had decided to stop looking back when she had agreed to marry Colin.

And now Colin was being accused of heaven-only-knew-what. Where on earth could he have got to? she wondered anxiously. He was the sort to take a small mistake terribly seriously. Was he out there somewhere in the cold and rain, afraid to come home, worrying about what he had done? She could only hope that he wouldn't do something stupid. . .

At least her concern for him should provide her with some sort of armour against the unnerving effect Saul Rainer had on her, she reassured herself as she carried Emma back downstairs—but even so she had to pause for a few seconds and draw in a deep, steadying breath before she could open the door.

He looked decidedly out of place, sitting there in her shabbily comfortable front room; the cut of his suit, the soft black leather of his handmade shoes hinted subtly but unmistakably at his wealth. Colin didn't talk much about his work, but she had a pretty good idea of the size of the Rainer empire; there had to be a branch of one of their electrical superstores in just about every high street and shopping mall in the country, selling everything from hair-dryers to computers. The company's turnover had to be in the millions—it was hardly surprising that the odd mistake could be made now and then.

Emma must have picked up some of her tension;

usually she was quite good with strangers, but she took one look at Saul Rainer and promptly buried her face in Shelley's shoulder, clinging around her neck with her chubby little arms. Shelley made no attempt to persuade her otherwise, but moved over to sit down in the armchair beside the fireplace, cooing to her softly.

Saul was watching her, a sardonic glint in those deep-set dark eyes. It must seem a little bizarre to him, she acknowledged with a touch of dry humour, to see this skinny bird in black, with her jangling earrings and purple nails, with a child in her arms—she got the same sort of curious looks when she walked down the road with Emma in her pushchair, or took her to the clinic. But looking different didn't stop you being a good mother.

'So this is your daughter?' he remarked, coolly polite.

'That's right. Emma, say hello.' But the child wouldn't have any of it, clinging fiercely around her neck.

'Colin has a photo of her on his desk—as well as one of you.'

'Does he?' There had been a note of cynicism in that dry voice. She couldn't imagine that family photos would feature on Saul Rainer's desk; not that he had a family, so far as she knew. But it was just like Colin to have them—he was the family type.

'She isn't his child, though, is she?' Saul enquired, still very formal.

'No.' Shelley shook her head, choosing not to elucidate any further.

'How long, exactly, have you been married?'

Was this some kind of interrogation? 'Seven weeks.' Absently she twisted the slim gold ring on the third finger of her left hand. 'We didn't even have a proper honeymoon because he didn't want to take the time off work,' she added with a touch of asperity.

That hard mouth conceded a humourless smile. 'I'm sorry—I wasn't aware that I was responsible for spoiling the romantic occasion.'

She dismissed the apology with a casual shrug of her slim shoulders, refusing to allow herself to be needled. To be honest, it hadn't exactly been a romantic wedding anyway; it had poured with rain, and the register office was a pretty dismal place on the best of days. The only bright spot had been her stepmother's unstinting approval of Colin—she had always regarded Luke as only one step removed from the devil incarnate.

Saul was watching her with that dark, disturbing gaze, and she wondered if he could read her thoughts. 'So, you're telling me that you really have no idea where your husband could be?' he queried, returning to the purpose of his visit.

'No, I'm afraid I don't.' And she had no reason to feel defensive, she reminded herself firmly—she had done nothing wrong, and, so far as she knew, Colin hadn't either.

'What about family, friends?' Saul persisted obdurately.

She shook her head. 'Colin doesn't know many people in England. He grew up in New Zealand—his family emigrated there when he was three. He only came back last September, after his mother died.'

'I see.' He seemed to be filing the information away in some mental card index. 'So you hadn't known him very long before you were married?'

'Not very long,' she conceded tautly.

'How long?'

'A. . .about six weeks.'

He lifted one dark eyebrow in frank surprise. 'As little as that? I wouldn't have thought Colin had it in him.'

She returned him a frosty glare, her hackles rising in swift defensiveness. 'And what exactly do you mean by that?'

That hard mouth curved into a slow smile. 'Well, he doesn't exactly strike me as the type to sweep a girl off her feet,' he remarked, that dark gaze sliding down over her in an insolent assessment that made her skin prickle. 'Particularly a girl like you.'

To her chagrin, she felt her cheeks heated by a betraying blush of pink. He was uncomfortably close to the truth. . . But she hardly cared to admit that to herself, so she certainly wasn't going to admit it to Saul Rainer. 'You're. . .very quick to jump to conclusions,' she parried defiantly.

'Perhaps,' he conceded, with a shrug of his wide shoulders that eloquently conveyed his doubt. 'Perhaps he's an entirely different person when he's away from the office. Does that Harley-Davidson out front under the tarpaulin belong to him?'

A familiar lump rose to her throat. 'No,' she responded with difficulty. 'That belonged to. . .Luke. My first husband—Emma's father. He was. . .restoring it. He used to own the motor-bike shop on the high street, next to the tube station. He. . .died nearly two years ago.'

'I see. I'm sorry.'

The unexpected note of sympathy in his voice almost caught her off-guard, and she was instantly on the defensive. 'Why should you be?' she countered frostily, determined to keep up the barrier of hostility between them. 'You never knew him. It was someone like you that killed him—someone respectable, driving a nice big car that kept him safe so he didn't have to bother to look out too much for anything else that happened to be on the road. Did you know that eighty per cent of motor-bike accidents are caused by car drivers? Only unfortunately, a motor-bike always comes off worse.'

'I know,' he agreed evenly. 'I used to ride one myself, until I got knocked off and broke my leg. Then I promised my mother I wouldn't get another one.'

'Oh. . .' Well, that had taken the wind out of her sails! 'I'm sorry—I. . .didn't know that.'

'So now who's jumping to conclusions?' he taunted, smiling in lazy mockery.

Without warning her heart skidded and began to beat much too fast. No wonder he had such a reputation with women, she reflected, a little dazed, if just one smile could have such a devastating effect!

Those dark eyes were watching her, much too perceptive. 'Why did you marry Colin?' he asked softly.

The question caught her off guard, and she found it difficult to retain enough control of her voice to speak. 'Because I. . .love him, of course,' she asserted, struggling to evade that compelling gaze. 'Besides, there was Emma,' she added with awkward honesty. 'She needed a father, and. . .well, Colin was always very good with her. There aren't many men who'd be so willing to take on another man's child.'

'True,' he acknowledged, a sardonic inflection in his voice. 'No doubt it was very noble of him.'

Shelley's eyes flashed green fire; she was wishing now that she hadn't told him so much—she might have guessed she would get a cynical response. 'Are you married?' she countered, distantly polite.

He shook his head. 'I've never got around to it.'

She wasn't surprised by his reply. From what she knew of him—from what she had read about him in the papers, what she had seen that evening at the office party—he wasn't the type to settle for cosy domesticity. He would prefer a more sophisticated relationship, unencumbered by the demands of a small child.

Emma, however, had no such reservations. For the past five minutes she had been regarding him with saucer-shaped blue eyes, but now she had apparently decided that he wasn't a great big green furry monster after all. With an insistent wriggle she clambered down from Shelley's lap and trotted across to flirt outrageously with him, grasping at his immaculately pressed trousers with her plump little hands and bouncing up and down, gurgling with laughter.

'Oh, I'm sorry,' Shelley apologised, moving quickly to retrieve her daughter. 'I hope she hasn't made a mess of them.'

'It's quite all right,' he assured her coolly, brushing down the razor-sharp creases. He regarded the child with detached interest. 'She looks very like you.'

'A lot of people say that. Though she's got her father's eyes,' she added on an unconsciously wistful note.

He watched her in silence for a moment, and then rose easily to his feet. 'Well, I'm sorry to have taken so much of your time, Mrs Clarke. I was hoping you would be able to shed some light on your husband's disappearance, but clearly you know as little as I do. I'd better let you put the little one to bed.'

'Yes, I. . . Thank you,' she stammered, guiltily aware of the rapid acceleration of her heartbeat as she looked up at him; she was a married woman, she reminded herself for about the twentieth time—she wasn't supposed to react to him like that. With an effort of will, she managed to regain control of her voice. 'How much money, exactly, is missing, Mr Rainer?' she enquired.

That hard mouth curved into a wry smile. 'I. . .don't really think I should worry you with that at the moment,' he demurred. 'It may well turn out to be nothing at all.'

She glanced at the clock on the mantelpiece; it was almost half past eight. 'It's serious enough to make my husband extremely late home,' she responded tautly. 'I really think I'd prefer to know.'

He hesitated, studying her slender frame. She returned his gaze levelly; she knew she looked delicate, but it took a certain amount of guts to pilot a powerful Harley-Davidson through the uncaring London traffic. He seemed to recognise that underlying hint of steel, because finally he nodded.

'At the moment, it's a little over fifty thousand pounds, but I'm afraid it could be more,' he told her baldly.

'I see.' For a moment she felt a little sick; it was an awfully large amount of money to lose by mistake. But then, after all, in the context of the turnover of the Rainer empire. . .

'I don't suppose there's any point telling you not to worry, Mrs Clarke,' he added. 'This is my private telephone number, and the number of the direct line into my office.' He handed her a small white square of card. 'If your husband returns, whatever time it is, please ask him to call me at once. And if you should hear anything. . .'

She swallowed hard. 'I'll ring you,' she concluded for him. 'Of course, he could have had an accident, or been taken ill. Perhaps I should try ringing the hospitals, and the police.'

'If something like that had happened, you would have been informed already,' he pointed out. 'He would have had some kind of identification on him.'

'Yes, I suppose so. Unless. . .' She bit her lip.

'For what it's worth, I don't think he's the kind to commit suicide,' he told her, a surprisingly gentle note in his voice.

'No.' She shook her head swiftly. 'No, I'm sure he's not.' He wouldn't do that to her, not knowing that she was only just beginning to get over Luke; to be widowed a second time, so soon, would be almost unbearable. 'But, even so, I ought to report him missing.'

He shook his head. 'Leave it till tomorrow. The police don't consider a person missing until they've been gone for twenty-four hours.'

'But in the circumstances—?'

'Particularly in these circumstances, Mrs Clarke. I don't want to jump to any conclusions, and I don't want to take any potentially damaging action until I have a little more information—your husband may still show up, and he may have a perfectly reasonable explanation for what's happened.'

He sounded as if he was beginning to concede that possibility after all, and she lifted her eyes to search his. But instead she found herself intrigued by the gold flecks in their depths—almost mesmerised. . . Her heart gave a sharp thud, and she looked away again quickly, a faint blush of pink rising to her cheeks.

'Well, goodnight, then, Mrs Clarke.' She couldn't miss the dry note of mockery in his voice; he knew as well as she did what was going on beneath the polite surface of the conversation—and knew, too, that it was totally wrong.

'My name is Shelley,' she murmured awkwardly; she wasn't quite used to being called Mrs Clarke yet, after seven years of being Mrs Krasinski, and to hear it repeatedly from his lips made her feel. . .odd.

He held out his hand to her, and rather uncertainly she placed hers in it, hoping he would attribute the slight trembling to her anxiety about her husband—it *ought* to be due to anxiety about Colin, she reminded herself fiercely.

'Shelley, then. Is that short for Michelle?'

She shook her head. 'No. It's Shelley as in Percy Bysshe Shelley,' she explained for about the millionth time in her life. 'My mother was a romantic.'

'Ah. "Thy smiles before they dwindle make the cold air fire",' he quoted softly. 'I'm afraid he's generally a bit too florid for me.'

She blinked up at him in surprise—she wouldn't have expected him to be familiar with the lyrical poets. 'That's the way they liked them in those days,' she responded with an unsteady laugh, drawing her hand away, conscious that she had let him hold it for rather too long. 'Goodnight, Mr Rainer.'

'Saul.'

'Saul,' she conceded, a little uncomfortably—but, after all, she had insisted that he use her first name. Although that *was* rather different, she argued—he was the boss, she merely the wife of an employee. Not that she had ever believed in that sort of status thing. No, if she was absolutely honest with herself, it felt a little too. . .intimate to be on first-name terms with him.

'And remember, I don't care if it's the middle of the night—if Colin shows up, have him call me.'

The grim note in his voice was a salutary reminder of the reason for his visit. 'Of course,' she said, tucking the card under the phone. 'Goodnight.'

'Goodnight.'

He let himself out, closing the door behind him—but not before she had caught a glimpse of a long, curved, very distinctive sports-car bonnet at the kerb. She might have guessed he'd drive something like an Aston Martin, she mused with a hint of wry humour—it was the car

Luke would have had, if he could have afforded it. And if he could have given up his beloved Harley. It was a car that took a lot of handling—a real driver's car. Which would be why Saul Rainer had chosen it.

It bothered her that she found it so difficult to control her reaction to him; she had never met anyone who had quite that effect on her before. Of course, while Luke had been alive there had been no question. . . And there shouldn't be now, she reminded herself with a sharp stab of guilt—she was married to Colin.

Perhaps it was some excuse that half the female population seemed to suffer from the same affliction. It had little to do with his wealth, although his reputation for ruthlessness in his business dealings certainly added to the fascination. No, it was something that lay beneath that urbane exterior, some hint of raw male power that was an intrinsic part of him, bone-deep and unforced.

She had been conscious of it from the first moment she had met him, in that exclusive West End nightclub, a little over a month ago. The memory rose again in her mind—the memory she had tried so hard to suppress. She could almost hear the music playing, see the lights spinning above the crowded dance floor. . .

The room was a little too warm, and someone had lit a cigar, its pungent smoke stinging Shelley's eyes. She really was making an effort, for Colin's sake, to look as if she was enjoying herself, but it wasn't easy; everyone else at their table was at least ten years older than she, and they all knew each other, and were exchanging the kind of coded gossip that unwittingly excluded outsiders. Her smile was beginning to feel as if it was pinned in place by superglue.

She was watching the dancers, trying to appear casual,

but some strangely compelling force seemed to keep dragging her eyes back to the tall man on the far side of the dance floor. Saul Rainer. . .

Much against her will, she had to admit that she was intrigued by him. His name seemed to be in the papers all the time—if it wasn't another ruthless business deal, it was the racing-car team he sponsored, or some stunning model or actress he had been seen dating. And she couldn't help but overhear the giggling gossip in the ladies' room every time she slipped away for a few minutes' respite from the strain of the evening—most of his female employees, including those whom she would have thought old enough to know better, seemed to regard him in much the same light as a pre-adolescent regarded the latest teeny-bopper craze.

His reputation had, if anything, tended to prejudice her against him, and it was with a critical eye that she watched him circulating the tables, dispensing charm. Though she really couldn't fault him on his manners, she acknowledged wryly. He was working his way strictly through the order of precedence, dancing with all the wives in turn. She couldn't imagine that he was enjoying himself, but he was managing to make it look as if he was.

He was circling the floor now with Margaret, the middle-aged and rather plump wife of the chief account-ant, and apparently flirting with her quite outrageously, to guess from her girlish laughter. Somehow he was able to make all his partners look like good dancers, however clumsy—he had a natural sense of rhythm that seemed rather oddly at variance with the formally tailored dinner jacket he was wearing.

Suddenly it occurred to her that it would be her turn next to dance with him. Her heart gave an odd little thump, and started to race. She could hardly refuse, not without creating the kind of awkwardness that Colin wouldn't like. Absently she reached for her wineglass; she rarely touched alcohol, and so had been very cautious about how much she drank tonight, but now she gulped it down as if she were parched. Already he was bringing Margaret back to their table. . .

The tension was knotting her stomach as he paused to exchange some genial banter with the other occupants of the table. Almost compulsively she reached for the wine bottle and refilled her glass, downing it swiftly. No one else seemed to have noticed her action. . .except him. He slanted her a look of sardonic humour, holding out his hand in polite invitation.

'Mrs Clarke—may I have the pleasure. . .?'

She rose a little unsteadily to her feet, hoping that the subdued lighting would conceal the faint blush that was colouring her cheeks. They stepped out onto the floor, and he slipped his arms around her, not holding her too close. Even so, she was acutely aware of the lean, hard power of his body, of a faint, musky, male scent—not an aftershave but the unique scent of his skin. It was doing very strange things to her pulse rate. . .

'What's so fascinating about my tie?'

She looked up, startled. 'I beg your pardon?'

'That's quite all right.'

She sensed that he was mocking her, and her green eyes flashed him a fulminating glare. He lifted one dark eyebrow in surprise; apparently that wasn't the kind of reaction he was accustomed to. And no doubt he had been fooled by the demure flowered frock into thinking she was just some mousy little housewife, overawed by dancing with the exalted Saul Rainer.

Which was exactly the impression she had been trying all evening to create, she reminded herself sharply, lowering her lashes to evade that perceptive gaze. But she suspected that it was already too late—he had seen through her disguise. And when, almost imperceptibly, he drew her closer, she knew that she had no choice but to submit, or risk drawing unwelcome attention to herself.

'So you're Colin's wife?' he mused, a strange inflection in his voice.

'That's right,' she managed stiffly.

'Hmm. I have to admit you're. . .not quite what I was expecting.'

'Oh?' She returned him a level look, lifting an enquiring eyebrow in her turn. 'What were you expecting?'

A faintly sardonic smile hovered around the corners of his mouth. 'Oh, someone small and sweet, and limpid as spring water.'

'Well, I'm sorry to disappoint you,' she countered caustically.

'Oh, I'm not disappointed,' he murmured on a note of husky amusement. 'I'm not disappointed at all.'

He had let his hand slide slowly down the length of her spine to mould over the smooth curve of her *derrière*, using the cover of the crowded dance floor to hold her intimately against him—far more intimately than any man had the right to hold another man's wife. And as she struggled to control her racing heartbeat she was all too acutely conscious that with every ragged breath her breasts were being crushed against the hard wall of his chest.

She ought to be furious—he was using his position quite ruthlessly to force her to endure his attentions. Except she knew that he wasn't. It was entirely her own fault that she couldn't control her own unexpected reaction to him; he was simply picking up the signals she was giving out, and responding accordingly.

The only thing she could do was try to focus on the song that was playing, each familiar line of the lyrics a precious few seconds closer to the end of the dance— he surely wouldn't risk defying his own careful protocol by keeping her out here longer than that? The trouble was that it was one of her favourites, the sweeping harmonies intensely romantic—and somehow she knew that from now on, whenever she heard it, she would think of him. . .

It seemed like an eternity that she was held in that strangely inescapable embrace. But far too soon the music ended, and he had to let her go. 'Thank you, Mrs Clarke,' he murmured, the glint of sardonic amusement in those dark eyes belying the cool formality of his voice. 'That was for me the highlight of the whole evening.'

He led her back to the table, and Colin glanced up, smiling in innocent pleasure at the few meaningless comments Saul addressed to him. Shelley felt a sharp stab of annoyance. Had he seen nothing of what had been going on? Or was he just naïve?

No, not naïve, she reflected, shaking her head to dispel the disturbing memory—just too decent even to suspect that his boss would be so unscrupulous as to play forbidden games with an employee's wife. And much too decent to suspect that his wife of just two weeks was already lusting after another man. . .

And where on earth could he have got to? she wondered, her conscience nagging at her. He should have been home almost two hours ago. Was he out there in the cold, rainy night somewhere, worrying, afraid to come home and tell her that he'd probably lost his job? Fool—as if she'd care about that. They'd get by. She still had some of the money left from Luke's insurance, which had already paid off the mortgage on the house, and then there was the money from the sale of the motor-bike shop as well.

But Colin wasn't the sort who'd like the idea of living off his wife's money—he was old-fashioned like that. Sweet.

Emma had fallen asleep against her shoulder, her breath soft and warm against her neck as she snuggled in against her. 'Back to bed, miss,' Shelley murmured, carrying her carefully up the stairs. 'Don't worry; Daddy-Colin will be home safe soon—nothing will have happened to him.'

If only she could be reassured by her own words! But from the moment Saul Rainer had appeared on her doorstep she had been troubled by some strange kind of sixth sense, warning her of impending disaster.

CHAPTER TWO

SHELLEY hadn't expected to sleep at all, but she woke to the sound of the milk bottles arriving on the step, to find herself alone in the big bed. She lay for a few moments, staring at the empty pillow beside her, fragments of her dreams, strange and disturbing, tugging at the fringes of her waking consciousness.

But with an effort of will she pushed them from her mind—she had quite enough to worry about this morning. In spite of Saul's assurances, she had spent nearly an hour last night ringing round to all the hospitals in the area, but her enquiries had drawn a blank. The dismal sound of rain against the window made her shiver beneath the warm duvet. It was a little after six o'clock in the morning. Where had Colin spent the night? Surely not on the streets somewhere?

A chuckle from upstairs warned her that Emma was also awake, so with a yawn she slid out of bed and reached for her thick woollen dressing gown, sliding her feet into her slippers. She found her small daughter attempting to perform head-stands in the corner of her cot, and scooped her up in a snuggling hug. 'You poo!'

'Poo!' Emma giggled, wrinkling her small pink nose.

'Nappy change!' She swung her high in the air. 'Then breakfast, huh?'

'Dadda?'

Shelley smiled wryly. 'He's not here, sweetheart—I don't know where he is. Gone to the moon, maybe—like the cow. Where did the cow jump? Over the moon!'

'Over the moon.' Emma batted a small, podgy hand at the mobile above her cot, making it dance—and bringing a familiar lump to Shelley's throat. Luke had hung it there, cooing over his newborn daughter. . . So many memories, she sighed wistfully, but maybe at last they were beginning to lose their jagged edge, so that she could look back now with just a sad regret, rather than the raw pain that had been her companion for so long. . .

That realisation struck her with some surprise. When had it happened, that loosening of the bonds of the past? She hadn't been aware of it before. . .

It wouldn't have something to do with Saul Rainer, would it? the small, niggling voice of her conscience whispered slyly. She shook her head quickly in denial, but the question wouldn't go away; she was attracted to him in a way that she knew was wrong, but she didn't seem to be able to control it.

And there was no excuse. However disappointed she may have been in her marriage to Colin—and with a small sigh she acknowledged how very much she *had* been disappointed—she had gone into it with her eyes wide open. She had settled for security—she couldn't expect fireworks as well.

So, now that it appeared that Colin could be in serious trouble, she would stand by him, she vowed with grim determination—whatever had happened. He deserved that much from her, at least.

With Emma in a clean nappy, topped and tailed and dressed in a pair of yellow dungarees and a rainbow-coloured sweater, Shelley carried her down to the kitchen and popped her into her high chair, and went to fetch the milk in from the step. She had half wondered if she might find some sort of note from Colin slipped through the letter box, but there was nothing. Frowning, she went back to the kitchen and turned the radio on, tuning it into the local station—if anyone had turned up somewhere suffering from amnesia or something, there might be some news on that.

Maybe she could try ringing round the hospitals again—and then she would ring the police. It was all very well for Saul Rainer to advise her not to worry. Her husband had been missing for almost twenty-four hours, since he had left for work yesterday morning—it was time to start getting very worried indeed.

While Emma enjoyed the various forms of entertainment provided by a bowl of porridge, Shelley settled herself at the kitchen table with the stack of London telephone directories and the telephone, and began a second round of calling the casualty departments of every hospital where there seemed the remotest possibility he could have landed at, and then those that seemed even less likely.

But two hours later she had still drawn a complete blank. Cupping her chin in her hand, she tried to make herself think back, to remember anyone he might have mentioned—an old schoolfriend, a distant cousin—anyone who might have some clue about where he might have gone. But he had never talked much about people he knew—just places mostly: the farm in New Zealand where he had grown up, Wellington where he had studied for his accountancy exams. . .

The ring of the doorbell cut across her thoughts, and her heart thudded sharply against her ribs. Colin? The police? Her legs felt shaky as she rose to her feet and hurried out to the hall. But the tall, wide-shouldered silhouette behind the glass wasn't Colin, and she was ready to bet it wasn't a policeman either. Trying not to admit to herself that some treacherous part of her had been hoping he would be back, she opened the door.

'Mr Rainer. . .um. . .Saul. . .er. . .come in,' she invited unsteadily, her hand unconsciously gathering the buttoned front of her dressing gown closer to her throat.

Those dark eyes were hard again, filled with suspicion. 'Good morning, Mrs Clarke.' He greeted her with pointedly cool formality, in marked contrast to the slight easing she had sensed between them last night. He stepped into the small, narrow hall, seeming to fill it with his presence as she closed the front door behind him. 'I take it that you've heard nothing from your husband since last night?'

'No, I haven't. Er. . .come into the kitchen—Emma's just finishing her breakfast and I don't like to leave her alone in her high chair.' She led the way, uncomfortably aware as he followed her that her hair was unbrushed and her dressing gown not the most elegant of garments. 'I'm sorry about the mess,' she added, hurrying to fetch a piece of kitchen towel to mop up a dollop of porridge that had somehow reached as far as the middle of the big, cluttered pine table.

'Not at all,' he responded drily, his sardonic glance taking in the chaos that could reign in a household dominated by the needs of a small child. A far cry from the kind of smart, sophisticated world he was, no doubt, accustomed to, she reflected with a trace of wry self-mockery.

'Can I make you a cup of coffee?' she offered, struggling to match his cool indifference.

'Thank you.'

Emma, after regarding him solemnly for a few moments, had either recognised him or decided afresh that he was a friend, and generously offered him her porridgey spoon, which he took gingerly in his fingers.

'Er. . .where would you like me to put this?' he enquired.

'Oh, I'm sorry. It can go in the dishwasher—there, next to the washing machine.' With one foot she slid the basket of yesterday's laundry out of the way. 'Could you put her bowl in there too, before it lands on the floor?'

Those dark eyes conceded a glint of wry amusement as he obliged. 'Anything else?'

She returned him an apologetic smile. It was probably not what he was used to, being asked to clear up a toddler's breakfast things. 'I'm afraid the coffee's only instant—I do have a filter, but Emma tore up the filter papers last week and I haven't got round to getting another packet yet.'

'Instant will be fine,' he responded without expression, moving a pile of picture books from one of the chairs and sitting down. Emma, spotting her belongings, instantly stretched out a hand, grunting imperiously to indicate her demands. Saul frowned down at the pile helplessly. 'Which one does she want?' he asked.

'Give her the one with the blue hippopotamus on the front,' she suggested. '*Wait*, Emma—sticky fingers,' she added, fetching another piece of kitchen towel to wipe her daughter's face and hands. 'There—clean girl! Rub noses.' She bent over the giggling child as Emma lifted her face to share their special loving gesture, and wished she were not quite so aware of the man watching them with his dark, level gaze, an intruder who didn't belong in this comfortable domestic scene.

The kettle was boiling, and she poured the coffee, bringing it over to the table and sitting down opposite him. 'I didn't expect you to be round today—at least, not as early as this,' she remarked a little awkwardly.

'Didn't you?'

'Have you heard anything?' she asked, disconcerted by the chill in his manner.

He nodded. 'Nothing I wanted to hear. I'm afraid that figure I gave you last night was something of an underestimate. If you multiply by ten, you might get something a little closer to the amount that's missing.'

For a moment Shelley stared at him in shock. Perhaps she'd misheard him last night, or her memory wasn't clear—she could have sworn he'd said fifty thousand, which would make it. . . 'Half a million pounds?'

'At least there's nothing wrong with your arithmetic.' Those dark eyes were like chips of black ice. 'It's actually close to six hundred thousand, and I'm still counting.'

'But. . . How?' she demanded blankly.

He shrugged his wide shoulders in a taut, angry gesture. 'A bogus account, a series of computer transfers. . . He took advantage of the fact that the chief accountant was in hospital—and I'm beginning to wonder now if that was a coincidence.'

Her eyes widened in disbelief. 'You surely can't believe he made Gerald ill?' she protested.

'They haven't diagnosed what's wrong with him yet. I'm going to suggest they consider poison.'

'Oh, don't be ridiculous!' she snapped. '*Colin?* He wouldn't hurt a fly.'

'I must say he's been at great pains to project that impression,' he conceded. 'The quiet, respectable family man, with his pictures of his wife and child on his desk. That is, if you really *are* his wife?' he added on a note of sardonic query.

'Of course I'm his wife,' she protested, startled. 'Even if you think Colin might lie about it, why should I?'

'For all I know, you could be his partner in crime,' he

countered abrasively. 'The perfect camouflage—who'd ever suspect a newly married man of plotting such a risky enterprise? You could be in for a cut of the proceeds. I dare say you could do with the money—it can't be easy, trying to cope as a single parent.'

'You're crazy! I'll show you my marriage licence if you like—then maybe you'll believe me.' She jumped to her feet, and ran over to the drawer of the Welsh dresser where she kept all her papers. Rummaging through the pile of brown envelopes that constituted her filing system, she came to one marked 'Birth Certs. etc.' and pulled it out. 'There!'

He quirked one dark eyebrow as he took the folded paper she was holding out to him and cast a swift glance over it. 'I stand corrected,' he conceded drily. 'However, it was an. . .understandable misapprehension, don't you think?'

She felt a hot blush of pink rise to her cheeks. 'I don't know what you mean,' she parried, a betraying tremor in her voice.

That hard mouth curved into a sardonic smile as he let his dark gaze drift down over her, seeming to see right through the inelegant tartan dressing gown, making her feel naked. 'Oh, I think you do,' he taunted softly. 'I don't think you've forgotten the night we first met, any more than I have. You're a grown-up woman, not a naïve young girl—you know exactly what was going on between us.'

She drew in a deep breath, struggling to regain some control of her racing heartbeat. 'I'm. . .afraid you were mistaken if you thought *anything* was going on, Mr Rainer,' she countered with dignity. 'Look, I'm. . .going to get dressed now, and then I'm going down to the police station, to report Colin missing. If he wasn't at work yesterday, he's been gone for more than twenty-four hours now. I'm seriously worried.'

'I'll come with you,' he said grimly. 'I think I've allowed more than enough time for him to get in touch if he has some kind of explanation. I should tell you that I also intend to hire a firm of private investigators to look for him—not that I have any doubts about the efficiency of the police, but they have a great many other cases to deal with and they may not be able to attend to this one with quite the urgency I require.'

She stared at him, chilled by the impact of his words. Saul Rainer had a reputation for ruthlessness, and she had no doubt that he would be a very dangerous enemy. Colin had been a fool to cross him.

'I have to get dressed,' she forced out. 'Would you keep an eye on Emma for me for a few minutes? You can turn the television on for her—there's her favourite cartoon programme on in a minute.' She escaped from the room without waiting for his reply, hurrying up the stairs to her bedroom and closing the door behind her.

What she really needed was a few moments alone to think. Her mind was in a turmoil; it seemed unbelievable that Colin—respectable, reliable Colin—could have stolen half a million pounds. But it didn't seem very likely that you could lose that much money by mistake. . . And you couldn't steal it on impulse, either—it would have taken a considerable amount of planning.

But it still seemed ridiculous—she simply couldn't imagine Colin as a *criminal*. And as for that implication about the chief accountant's illness not being a coincidence. . . No, it was complete nonsense—there had to be another explanation.

Like, for instance, that Saul Rainer was lying.

A small, cold chill began to curl its fingers around her

heart. Could that be it? But why would he need to steal from his own company? Surely he couldn't be short of money? But then. . .he had a very expensive lifestyle, if half of what was written about him was true. Maybe he had diverted the money to defraud the other share-holders—and when he had feared that Colin would find out he could have decided to make him the scapegoat.

But why had Colin said nothing to her? she mused, frowning. And why had he disappeared, making it all the more likely that he would be seen as guilty? She moved over to sit down on the edge of the bed, which was still rumpled from her restless night's sleep. Poor Colin—he would be no match for a ruthless operator like Saul Rainer. If it *was* Saul who was responsible for the money going missing, Colin could be in very real danger.

And now Saul was here, in her house. Was he trying to find out how much she knew? All those searching questions. . . Perhaps that was why Colin had told her nothing—to protect her. If Saul thought she had any information that could incriminate him, she could be in danger too.

Absently she stroked her hand over the sheets—and with a sudden, vivid clarity the memory of last night's dreams flooded her mind, making her heartbeat race, conjuring disturbing images of two naked bodies, entwined. . .

She snatched her hand up as if she had been scalded. Somehow she had to try to keep a cool head—and letting herself indulge in those kinds of traitorous fantasies was not the way to do it. OK, so she couldn't be held respon-sible for the tricks her unconscious mind might play on her while she was asleep, but while she was awake she was going to have to keep them very strictly under con-trol. Because Saul Rainer had been right about one thing—she had known only too well what was going on that night when she had danced in his arms, and she had held the memory in some secret part of her mind ever since.

The trouble, she was forced to acknowledge, was that he had recognised right away that hint of ambivalence, as she was still trying to make herself believe she had done the right thing in marrying Colin. He was too damned perceptive—a skill honed through long practice in the art of seduction, no doubt. He could spot any hint of vulnerability, and knew exactly how to exploit it.

And though, as he had said, she was a grown-up woman—twenty-seven years old and married twice—she didn't have a lot of practice in dealing with men like him. Well, to be absolutely honest, none at all. She'd been seventeen when she had met Luke, and eighteen when she had married him, and Colin was the first man she had been out with since Luke had died. In the sense Saul Rainer was talking about, she might as well have still been a schoolgirl.

But if he thought he could play on that element of physical attraction to sway her judgement, he would find himself very much mistaken, she vowed grimly. Now, more than ever, she owed Colin her loyalty—if she didn't believe in his innocence, who would?

With that resolution firmly in her mind, she gathered up her clothes and went into the bathroom to wash and get dressed. Twenty minutes later, armoured in black with her hair clipped loosely back from her face and a pair of enamelled chandeliers swinging from her ears, she was ready to march downstairs and face the devil himself.

But as she walked into the kitchen, a breezy, 'Sorry I've been so long,' on her lips, she halted in shocked amazement. 'Hey—what do you think you're doing?' she demanded indignantly—though it was something of a rhetorical question. He was sitting at the kitchen table with the drawer from the dresser in front of him, calmly examining its contents. 'How dare you go through my things?'

He glanced up at her, coolly unconcerned. 'Do you have something to hide?'

'Of course I haven't!' she retorted, her eyes blazing. 'But you have no right to pry—and without even asking me!'

A glint of impatience flickered in his dark eyes. 'This is serious,' he countered. 'I don't have time for niceties.'

'What you mean is, you don't have the manners!' she shot back at him, furious. 'You think you're so damned important, you can just walk in here and do whatever you like!'

For one bristling moment they confronted each other across the table, but then Emma, alarmed by the sharp voices, gave a wail of distress, holding out her arms to her mother. Shelley plucked her out of her high chair, cuddling her close in comfort, shafting a fierce glare at Saul over the top of her golden head.

'Now look what you've done!' she accused bitterly. 'There, there, sweetheart—it's all right. Mummy wasn't cross with you.'

He returned her a look of sardonic mockery, perfectly well aware that she was using the child's distress to mask her own. But then he conceded a small smile. 'All right, I'm sorry,' he acknowledged. 'I should have asked you first. Now, do you mind if I look through these papers? There could be something in here that would give me some idea of where to begin to look for your husband.'

She hesitated, eyeing him with wary suspicion. If it

was Saul Rainer who had stolen the money, she should be doing everything she could to obstruct his search, to give Colin time to do whatever he needed to do to prove his innocence. The trouble was that she wasn't at all sure what she could do to prevent him.

'I doubt if you'll find anything, but you can look,' she said with frosty dignity. 'I'm afraid most of it's just rubbish I should have thrown away a long time ago—there must be gas bills in there dating back five years or more!'

'I've already discovered that,' he acknowledged with a flash of dry humour. 'I'll finish it off when we get back from seeing the police.'

Shelley nodded stiffly, checking Emma's nappy with her hand. 'You might as well carry on for a couple of minutes—I'll have to change her before we go out. I won't be long.'

She left him to it, and went off to sort Emma out, and to pack the capacious bag of necessities she always had to take with her—sometimes it seemed like taking an army on manoeuvres just to get to the shops. Then, with the child strapped securely into her buggy, she hooked her black leather biker's jacket down from behind the door and went back to the kitchen.

'OK, we're ready,' she announced breezily.

He lifted one quizzical eyebrow and rose to his feet, tossing down the sheaf of papers he had been looking through. 'At last. By the way, I take it you've got a photograph of him to show the police?'

She frowned, and shook her head. 'No, I don't—he took some of me and Emma at Christmas, but he wouldn't let me take one of him. He said he hated having his picture taken.'

'Don't you have any wedding photographs?'

'They. . .didn't come out. We didn't bother with a proper photographer—they just get in the way. So my stepbrother took some with Colin's camera, only there must have been something wrong with the film. . .'

'How very. . .unfortunate,' Saul commented drily. 'Or convenient, depending on which way you look at it.'

Shelley flashed him a look of sharp annoyance. 'I know—his passport!'

'Very good,' he acknowledged. 'Where is it?'

'In that drawer—or it should be.' She lifted questioning eyes to his. 'You didn't find it?'

He shook his head. 'Could it be somewhere else?'

'I don't know,' she temporised uncertainly. 'I'd have to search for it properly.'

'I very much suspect that you'd be wasting your time,' he surmised, his voice grim. 'I think we'd better get down to the police station.'

She nodded, part of her mind reluctantly beginning to concede that he could be right. It *did* seem a little too convenient, if you chose to look at it like that, that there wasn't a single photograph of Colin in the house. But if that was deliberate it would mean that he had been planning this as long ago as their wedding! She couldn't believe that. And yet. . .why would he have taken his passport out of the drawer?

As she turned to lead the way back up the hall, Saul gave a low whistle of approval. Instantly bristling, she flashed him a look of icy anger—and then blushed as she realised it wasn't her neat *derrière* in her short black skirt, nor her long, slender legs that he was admiring, but the Chinese dragon appliquéd to the back of her jacket.

'That's very good,' he remarked. 'Who did it?'

'I did.'

Those dark eyes glinted in mocking amusement. 'So—

you're a woman of many talents,' he taunted. 'I suspected the first time I saw you that you weren't quite the dull, conventional little housewife you were trying to pretend to be.'

'I wasn't trying to pretend to be anything,' she protested, her voice a little unsteady. 'I *am* a housewife.'

'But not exactly a conventional one,' he pointed out with a sardonic smile. 'They'd drum you out of the Women's Institute if you showed up in that nail varnish—not to mention those earrings.'

He touched one with the tip of his finger, lifting it to examine the colourful swirls of enamel paint. Shelley felt her mouth go dry. Having him stand so close, in the confined space of the narrow hall, she was much too aware of him—of the lean, hard-muscled frame beneath his immaculately tailored suit, of the faint, evocative, male scent of his skin. . .

His eyes moved to meet hers, and it was as if he was spinning some kind of spell around her, holding her prisoner. Her lips parted on a soundless sigh; she couldn't pretend, even to herself, that she hadn't been wondering for the past month what it would be like if he should kiss her.

But at that moment Emma, restless at being confined in her buggy, began to bounce vigorously, chattering to herself in an unintelligible gurgle. Drawing in a sharp breath, Shelley stepped back, stumbling over her own feet in her haste to escape, to deny what had so nearly happened. Saul shot out a hand to catch her arm, to steady her, and she snatched it away as if she had been scalded.

'Don't! Don't touch me!' she protested, retreating further down the hall.

'Oh?' He arched one dark eyebrow in quizzical

enquiry. 'That's not the message you were giving me a moment ago.'

She knew that it was true, but she certainly wasn't going to acknowledge it. 'My God, you really think you're irresistible, don't you?' she countered, choosing attack as the most effective mode of defence. 'In case you've forgotten, I'm. . .married.'

'Oh, I hadn't forgotten,' he responded, his voice low and husky. 'Married. How long is it? Just seven weeks?' His laughter was laced with biting mockery. 'It seems to me there's something just a little bit wrong with your marriage already, Mrs Clarke.'

'There isn't! Just leave me alone.' Stupid tears were stinging her eyes and she blinked them back. 'Colin and I are perfectly happy—*were* perfectly happy, until. . .all this business started up. And you haven't shown me a single shred of proof that he's done anything wrong,' she added fiercely. 'Until you do I shall. . .keep an open mind.'

'I admire your loyalty,' he said drily. 'What a pity it's being wasted on such an unworthy subject.' He glanced down at the buggy. 'You won't need that—we can go in my car.'

Somehow she managed to return him a look of cool enquiry. 'Oh? You have a child-seat in it?'

He conceded a wry smile. 'No, I don't,' he admitted.

'Then Emma and I will walk, thank you. It isn't far.'

'It's raining,' he pointed out quizzically.

'That's all right. A little rain won't wash us away.'

'That sounds like the sort of thing my mother used to say,' he taunted. 'All right—I'll walk with you.'

'I'd really rather you didn't!' she countered in alarm.

'Why?' His eyes glinted with dark amusement. 'Afraid the neighbours will be twitching their net curtains, thinking they've come across a nice juicy bit of scandal?'

'I couldn't care less about the neighbours,' she retorted. 'It's just. . .'

'What?' he queried mockingly. 'That you're afraid to walk down the street with me? You think I might drag you into the bushes and ravish you? If I was going to ravish you, I'd be much more likely to do it right here, don't you think?' He smiled slowly, watching the hot blush of pink steal up over her cheeks. 'Would you like me to?' he mocked, his voice taking on a huskier timbre. 'I'd be more than willing, you know. I have a feeling that making love with you would be quite. . .memorable.'

She had to struggle to maintain some semblance of composure, her eyes flashing him a frost warning. 'Do you make a habit of behaving like this with married women?' she demanded.

'No.' He shook his head, untroubled by her barbs. 'In that respect, you're quite unique. As it happens, I have a great deal of respect for the institution of marriage, even though it's never attracted me personally. But you really shouldn't be married to Colin,' he added with a smile of sardonic humour. 'Try as I might, I just can't picture you with him.'

'You saw me with him at the office party,' she reminded him tautly—it was becoming harder and harder for her to picture herself with Colin.

'So I did,' he mused reminiscently. 'And you didn't look right with him, even then. Even in that silly, dowdy dress you were wearing, you made me look at you. I had to dance with practically every other damned woman in the room before I could dance with you—I was afraid you'd leave before I got to you. But when I finally did get to dance with you it was worth the wait. You looked up at me with those witchy green eyes, and you moved against me as if we were making love right there in the middle of the dance floor. Every time I've thought about it since, it's made my mouth water.'

It made Shelley's mouth water too, shocked as she was at the realisation that she had made such an impact on him. But she knew what he was trying to do—he was trying to use that helpless attraction she felt to undermine her judgement, to lure her into his treacherous coils and persuade her to turn against Colin, to believe that he really had done something wrong.

It took every ounce of will-power she possessed to control the unsteady beating of her heart, but she managed it. 'Forget it, Mr Rainer,' she advised tartly. 'Even if I wasn't married, I wouldn't be interested. I don't go in for. . .that sort of thing.'

'And what sort of thing is that?' he countered, a sardonic inflection in his voice.

'Casual sex,' she returned with icy dignity. 'That's what you're talking about, isn't it? Oh, I have no doubt you have an excellent *technique*.' She made it sound like an insult. 'It's just that, for me, there would always be something lacking.'

His smile was lazily mocking. 'Very creditable,' he accorded, his dark eyes sliding down over her in a way that heated her blood like a fever. 'But if you're trying to tell me that you're satisfied in your relationship with Colin, I'm afraid I'm not going to believe you. I can see it in your eyes every time you look at me. You need more than he can give you—a *lot* more.'

'You have a very colourful imagination,' she retorted crisply, turning an aloof shoulder to him and taking hold of the buggy, leaning across it to unfasten the door. 'There's absolutely nothing I want that you could give me.'

'No?' The husky sound of his laughter wrapped around her like a caress. 'Oh, I'm sure we could think of something.'

'Hell might freeze over first!'

CHAPTER THREE

THEY were at the police station for rather longer than Shelley had expected; it had taken most of the morning to give them her statement, and she could sympathise with Emma's hungry protests as they finally found themselves back out in the street. She hesitated on the pavement, assessing the rival merits of the fifteen-minute walk home *vis-à-vis* the brightly coloured fast-food emporium on the corner.

Her stomach made the decision for her. 'Would you like chicken nuggets for lunch, Emma?' she suggested, turning the buggy in that direction. She slanted a swift glance up at Saul. 'Well, goodbye, then,' she managed, her voice commendably even. 'I'll let you know if I hear anything else.'

Those dark eyes glinted in mocking amusement. 'You're going in there to eat?' he queried. 'I think I'll join you; I could do with something myself.'

'In there?' She glanced from him, in his immaculately tailored business suit, to the Dayglo plastic of the bar, with its Formica tables and nattily dressed counter assistants.

'Why not? It's well past lunchtime. And then afterwards I'll come back to your house, if I may, and finish looking for anything that could tell us where Colin could have gone.'

Shelley would have liked to be able to refuse. She still didn't trust him, and she would have preferred not to have to spend any more time in his company. But she

was quite sure he wouldn't find anything incriminating—
and if Colin had wanted her to protect him he should
have told her what was going on, instead of leaving her
to cope with Saul Rainer on her own.

'A. . .all right,' she conceded grudgingly, nodding her
thanks as he held the door open for her.

The place wasn't too busy, and they were soon settled
at a corner table, Emma in a high chair with a plate of
chicken nuggets in front of her which she was happily
eating with her fingers. Shelley took a large bite out of
her burger, glancing across at Saul as he did the same
with his.

'So, tell me everything you know about Colin,' he said.
'We might be able to figure something out between us.'

She lifted her slim shoulders in a casual shrug. 'I don't
really know a great deal,' she admitted. 'He never talked
about himself very much. He was born in Hampshire,
and adopted by a couple who had a farm. I don't think
they actually owned it—they were just tenants or something. Anyway, when Colin was three they emigrated to
New Zealand, and his father started farming out there—
dairy cattle. Colin was in his teens when his father died,
and he and his mother moved to the city. She died last
year—that's when he decided to come back to England.'

'He was an only child?'

'So far as I know.'

'You don't seem to know an awful lot about him,' he
remarked, a sardonic inflection in his voice. 'And yet
you were prepared to take the chance of marrying him?'

She found herself bridling defensively. 'Yes, I did!
You don't need to know every detail about someone's
past history, you know.'

'I'll take your word for that,' he responded drily.
'You're more of an expert on the subject of matrimony

than I am. So if he didn't talk about himself, what did he talk about?'

'Oh, you know—the usual things. . .' It was odd, but now she came to think about it she couldn't remember anything much they had talked about.

'Such as?' Saul persisted.

'Well. . .films, or what was on television, I suppose. The news. . .'

'Goodness, what a breathlessly exciting life,' he drawled on a note of lazy mockery. 'I suppose he never mentioned any previous girlfriends, anything like that?'

'No, he didn't!' she retorted hotly.

'He sounds as if he practically sprang into existence some time last September,' Saul mused, stirring his coffee. 'And now, having no photographs of him, it's as if he never was. Except for my missing money, of course.'

Shelley was forced to acknowledge the uncomfortable truth of that. She picked up the tiny plastic paddle that was supposed to serve as a spoon and absently stirred her coffee, although there wasn't any sugar in it. It almost seemed as if they were talking about a stranger, not the Colin she knew—or had thought she knew. The evidence certainly seemed to be mounting up against him. 'How did he get the job with your company?' she asked.

'The usual way—through an advertisement in the Press.' He frowned, his mouth a grim line. 'I shall have to tighten up on my personnel department's procedures. Although it does seem that he was properly qualified— that was checked.'

'Surely he must have had references as well?'

He shrugged his wide shoulders, leaning back in his seat. 'They seemed perfectly in order at the time— they're being followed up again.'

She nodded, frowning. 'Why do you think he may have done it?' she queried, beginning to allow the possibility. 'Do you think he may have had some kind of grudge?'

'It's possible—although I don't think so. I'm afraid it looks as if it was just pure greed. He was dealing with vast amounts of money—maybe he just saw an opportunity to divert some of it his own way. It could well have started out as quite a small thing—just the odd decimal point from each transaction re-routed into an unauthorised holding account. But, once the computer had been programmed to do it, it would have started to mount up—perhaps more quickly than he had anticipated. Then when he realised that it was coming to the end of the financial year and the accounts were due for audit he realised it would all be uncovered, so he panicked and ran.'

'And Gerald?'

He smiled wryly. 'I don't know—it could just have been a coincidence that he became ill at the same time. That could even have been the root of it. As you said, Colin was under a lot of pressure, coping with Gerald's work as well as his own—maybe he made some kind of mistake, and then when he realised what was happening he was tempted to just let it carry on. He wouldn't be the first newly married man to find himself overwhelmed by the financial responsibility of caring for a family,' he added with a touch of cynicism.

'Oh, you think it was *my* fault now?' Shelley retorted, her eyes flashing green sparks. 'You think I was the type of wife who was forever demanding new fitted carpets, or a wardrobe full of shoes? Well, for your information, if I wanted those things I could buy them for myself— Luke took care of that. I don't need a meal-ticket. . .'

A well-aimed splodge of chicken nugget, landing on the tiled floor, provided a welcome distraction.

'No, Emma, *don't* throw your food,' she scolded, stooping to scoop up the mush with a paper napkin. It had probably been unnecessary to bite at him like that, but telling herself to be sensible around him seemed to do no good at all. Her emotions had been on a permanent roller coaster from the moment Saul Rainer had walked into her life.

Emma, her chubby tummy now replete, was busy discovering the artistic potential of chicken nuggets, squidging the remnants of her meal through her fingers and dabbing them all over the tray of the high chair.

'What a mess!' Saul remarked, smiling in amusement at the child's intense concentration on her game. 'Still, she seems to be enjoying herself. How old is she?'

'Just over twenty-two months,' Shelley told him, moving the plate out of Emma's way and briskly wiping her face and hands with a wet-wipe fished out of the bottomless bag. 'There—good girl.'

'Good girl,' Emma echoed with satisfaction, nodding her golden-blonde head. She had seemed unaware of Saul for the past half-hour, but now, her games with her dinner forgotten, she had apparently decided to turn her attention to enchanting this new man who had appeared so recently on her horizon, favouring him with all the dazzling power of her peg-toothed smile. Then she spotted the bright metal gleam of his watch beneath the white cuff of his shirt, and reached out an insistent hand to plead for it.

'What does she want?' Saul queried, puzzled.

Shelley laughed. 'Your watch. You little tinker,' she scolded affectionately, buffing the child's rosy cheek. 'Are you in training to be a gold-digger? No, don't let her play with it,' she added in alarm as Saul began to slip the watch from his wrist. 'She'll probably throw it on the floor.'

He smiled wryly, refastening the catch. 'It's supposed to be shock-proof, but I don't think I'll chance it! Thanks for the warning—I'm not really very used to kids of that age.'

'I can see that,' she responded with a touch of dry humour. 'Try giving her your car keys to play with—she loves them.'

'The keys to an Aston Martin?' he queried, arching one quizzical eyebrow as he fished them from his pocket and jangled them for the little girl, letting her reach out to clasp them. 'Aren't you afraid of encouraging her gold-digging tendencies?'

'I'm hoping to raise her aspirations so she'll want to get one for herself,' she returned, her eyes dancing.

He laughed, watching in fascination as Emma investigated the keys in minute detail, turning them over and around, examining the fob, sticking her small fingers through the loop of the keyring, and finally trying out the taste.

Across the table, Shelley studied him with covert interest, intrigued by the slight softening in his features as he responded, still a little awkwardly, to her small daughter's captivating charm. He had none of Colin's easy jollity with the little girl—she couldn't even begin to imagine him pulling faces, or making puppets with his fingers—but strangely Emma seemed to like him anyway.

If she had met him under any other circumstances, maybe things could have been different. If she hadn't been married. . . But that was just a foolish dream, the voice of common sense chided her. Whatever the circumstances, there was no future for her in a relationship with

Saul Rainer. He was the type to whom everything in life came too easily—money, women. . .whatever he wanted. And, like a child with too many toys, what came easily he would quickly tire of; he would always be on the lookout for a new game, a new challenge—whether it was another company to take over, or another woman.

Apart from which, she *was* married, she reminded herself with a sharp stab of reproach. Which perhaps explained why he seemed to be interested in her, though she was nothing like the type of woman he was usually seen with, if the stories in the tabloids were even half right. But she had a certain novelty value—the attraction of the unattainable. If she had been free, he probably wouldn't have looked twice in her direction.

With an effort, she managed to return to the previous topic of conversation, enquiring in a light tone, 'Don't you have any nieces or nephews?'

He shook his head. 'I never had any brothers or sisters,' he responded. 'I was a "lonely only"—isn't that the expression?'

She slanted him a questioning glance, her curiosity caught by this unexpected glimpse of the man behind the cool public façade. 'You were a lonely child?'

The façade was swiftly back in place as he dismissed the question with a casual shrug of his wide shoulders. 'Not particularly—what you've never had you never miss. Are you planning to have more children?'

She felt her cheeks flush a hot scarlet. 'I. . .haven't really thought about it yet,' she managed to respond. 'I certainly won't have one just so Emma isn't an only child—there's nothing wrong with that so long as they have other children to play with, and brothers and sisters don't necessarily get on with each other.'

But growing up as an only child could give you that

kind of self-sufficiency that put up walls against other people, she reflected—or made you think that you didn't need anyone else. . .

But she wasn't supposed to be letting herself take an interest in Saul Rainer's personal history, she reminded herself crisply—she was supposed to be keeping him firmly at arm's length. She glanced up at the big play-face clock on the wall. 'I'd better be getting home,' she remarked, a little surprised to see how long they had been sitting there. 'This little minx will need her nap or she'll start getting grizzly again.'

'OK.' Saul rose to his feet, holding out his hand to Emma for his keys. 'Thank you,' he said as she handed them to him. The child looked up at him in mild surprise—it was the first time he had actually spoken directly to her. This development was sufficient for her to decide that he—and he alone—should lift her down from her high chair.

'Go on,' Shelley urged, amused by his awkwardness.

With a slightly crooked smile, he put his hands around the child's middle and slid her out of the high chair, swinging her up over his head. She squealed in delight, wriggling insistently as he lowered her down, so he did it again, laughing back at her. 'You little demon!' he teased her. 'You'd have me doing this all day, wouldn't you?'

'You've got it,' Shelley confirmed drily. 'Come on, Emma—buggy.'

The little girl shook her head vigorously. 'Emma push it!' she demanded.

'That's fine by me!'

Gratefully Shelley swung her capacious shoulder bag down onto the buggy seat to provide a counterbalance as Emma reached up to grasp the handlebar, which was slightly above the level of her forehead, and surged forward with the rolling gait of a land-bound sailor. She reached the door with rather more luck than judgement, and Shelley had to grab at the buggy swiftly to stop her from banging it against the glass as Saul leaned across and opened it for them.

'Thank you,' she murmured as she stepped past him.

'Oh, excuse me, sir.' The young lad who was clearing the tables hurried up, holding out Emma's juice cup to Saul. 'Your wife left this.'

Saul hesitated, and then took the cup from him as warily as if it had been a hand-grenade. 'Thank you,' he responded flatly.

Shelley slanted him a wry glance from beneath her lashes. His reaction was a timely reminder—if she had needed one—that the past hour in the café had been no more than a temporary interlude. Saul Rainer was not the family-man type—she really couldn't imagine him as anyone's husband, let alone anyone's father.

And even if she could, she reminded herself sharply, he could never be for her. Apart from anything else, she was already married. It was a little ironic, really, that it was only through Colin that she had met him—and through Colin's disappearance that she was seeing so much of him.

And she still didn't know for sure that it wasn't Saul Rainer who was responsible for that disappearance. After all, there was no real proof yet that Colin had stolen the money—all the evidence was purely circumstantial. So much for keeping an open mind, for waiting to hear Colin's side of the story, she acknowledged with an uncomfortable twinge of conscience; she had let herself be beguiled by Saul Rainer's easy charm, until she was more than half believing that Colin really had done exactly what he was being accused of.

But right now Emma was striding off along the pavement with a total disregard for the principles of the Highway Code, wielding the buggy like a small Chieftain tank. Shelley hurried to catch her; later she would sit down and rationally try to weigh up the evidence she had so far, but at this moment it was more important to prevent an outbreak of damaged ankles among the innocent pedestrians being scattered into the kerb.

It took Saul more than an hour to work systematically through the contents of the kitchen drawer, but he didn't find anything to give a clue to Colin's whereabouts. 'Nothing!' he declared at last. 'Not a single thing.'

Shelley, who had been getting on with her ironing while Emma had her nap, folded the last small T-shirt and added it to the pile; the only thing left now was Colin's shirts, and she didn't quite feel inclined to do those at the moment. 'So?' she queried, turning off the iron, and putting it on its stand to cool and collapsing the ironing board.

'So. . .why not?' Saul mused, half to himself. 'Any normal person would have all sorts of personal junk tucked away—old receipts, letters. . . But there's nothing in this lot to say that he even existed—nothing to tell me anything at all about his life.'

Shelley came over and sat down on one of the other chairs, surveying the neat piles he had made of the chaos that had existed before. 'Well, at least you've tidied it up for me,' she remarked drily. 'I've been meaning to do that for ages.'

'I'm glad to have been of service,' he retorted, an inflection of sardonic humour in his voice.

She propped her elbow on the table, dropping her chin onto her hand. 'I suppose it *does* seem a little odd,' she conceded with a small sigh. 'Though I find it very hard to picture Colin as some kind of master criminal.' She forced a crooked smile. 'Though I suppose if he'd looked like Al Capone I wouldn't have married him in the first place.'

'Why *did* you marry him?' he queried softly.

'I. . .I told you. Because I. . .love him. . .' But her protest didn't sound convincing even to her ears. Summoning every ounce of will-power she possessed, she rose to her feet. 'Would you like another cup of coffee?' she enquired briskly, though all her best efforts weren't quite able to keep her voice level.

'Thank you.' His voice had a faintly ironic note, as if he knew how determined she was to keep the barriers between them.

She moved across the room to put the kettle on, a little too conscious of him watching her. Why was it so difficult to keep reminding herself that he didn't belong here? He was as out of place in her world as she would be in his—they might as well come from different planets.

'When did you meet Luke?' he asked in a conversational tone.

She slanted a glance back at him, trying to guess whether this was anything more than polite interest. 'I was still at school—in the sixth form. He was one of a gang of bikers who used to hang around our local coffee-bar, and we used to go there after school. My stepmother used to go ape about it—she was a real lace-doilies-on-the-table, knitted-poodles-over-the-toilet-rolls type.'

'Knitted poodles?' he repeated, bemused.

'That's right.' She gurgled with laughter. 'She made them herself—a pink one and a blue one, side by side

on the bathroom window-sill. You've never seen anything so ghastly in your life.'

'I can imagine!' he conceded weakly.

'Anyway, she threatened all sorts of things when she
found out I was going out with Luke. She even went to
see a solicitor about getting me made a ward of court,
but of course he told her that there was nothing she could
do—I was old enough to leave home if I wanted to.'

'And what did your father make of all this?' Saul
queried, leaning back in his chair and propping his foot
lazily on a rung of Emma's pushchair.

'Oh, he always went along with whatever she said,'
Shelley responded with a touch of asperity. 'All he
wanted was a quiet life, bless him.'

'What happened to your mother?' he asked.

Shelley unscrewed the coffee-jar, spooning the
granules into a couple of mugs, and then went to fetch
the milk from the fridge. 'She died when I was seven,'
she told him, her voice flat. 'Dad married Eileen a couple
of years later.'

'And you didn't like it?'

She shook her head, smiling wryly. 'Oh, it wasn't that
bad. Eileen's nice enough in her own way, and she's
been good to Dad, even if she does tend to bully him a
bit—mostly for his own good. And she's very fond of
Emma—in a way that's brought us closer, though we
still don't see eye to eye on most things. Particularly the
clothes I wear.'

'Well, no.' He let his eyes slide down over her,
reflecting a hint of sardonic amusement. . .and something
else, something infinitely more dangerous. 'I can see how
someone who puts pink and blue poodles on her toilet
rolls might find your choice of wardrobe a little. . .alien.'

'It's my business what I wear,' she insisted, struggling

to control the sudden acceleration of her heartbeat.

'I didn't say it wasn't,' he said on a note of lazy mockery. 'And I'm not complaining either—you look fine to me. The earrings take a little getting used to,' he added judiciously, 'but even those are beginning to grow on me.'

Shelley could feel a hot blush of pink stealing into her cheeks, and quickly turned her attention to the kettle, which had started to boil. No doubt he found it amusing to try to flirt with her like this, but she wasn't amused. It stirred up responses inside her that made her feel uncomfortable—made her want things she shouldn't want, knew she couldn't have.

She made the coffee and brought it back to the table, setting his mug down in front of him with a certain amount of force. He glanced up at her, one dark eyebrow lifted in sardonic enquiry, but he made no comment, simply leaning back in his chair until it was tipped onto its back legs, regarding her with that strange, enigmatic smile.

'Well, so. . .what happens now?' she demanded, flustered by the way he was looking at her.

He shrugged. 'It might be useful if I could take a look around the rest of the house, if that's OK with you.'

'Why should I object?' she countered tautly. 'Tear up the floorboards, why don't you? Just try to do it tidily—I don't fancy spending the next week clearing up after you.'

'I'll do my best,' he responded with a bland smile. 'I might as well start at the top and work my way down. Do you have an attic?'

'Yes, but it's pretty dusty up there,' she warned him, slanting a dubious eye over his expensively tailored suit. 'I'm not one of those housewives who flits around her nooks and crannies with a feather-duster every other day.'

Those dark eyes glinted with provocative humour. 'Now, there's a thought,' he murmured, deliberately reading a much saucier interpretation into her words, making her cheeks once again blush a heated red. He laughed softly. 'You know, there can't be many women of your age, twice married, who can blush as easily as you do,' he taunted.

'I'm not doing it deliberately,' she threw back at him. 'I'd really prefer not to. No doubt the kind of women you're accustomed to can bandy that kind of remark with you all the time, but. . .I'm not. Don't forget, I got married at eighteen to my first proper boyfriend, and I was married to him for seven years or so. I haven't exactly led a wild life, in spite of appearances.'

'Then maybe it's time you started,' he suggested, his voice low and sensuously teasing.

She shook her head, refusing to listen to the treacherous whisper of temptation in her heart. 'No, thank you,' she asserted firmly. 'For one thing, I *am* married—whatever Colin may have done. And we don't know for sure that he's done anything yet,' she added, struggling to recapture her earlier doubts. 'OK, the money's missing and he's missing, but the two may not even be connected.'

'That's a bit of a long shot,' he pointed out drily.

'It probably is,' she acknowledged, guiltily aware of just how much she had allowed herself to be swayed from the loyalty she owed her husband. 'But I'm still his wife, and I have no intention of. . .being unfaithful to him. And besides, there's Emma,' she continued more surely. 'I can't go sowing my wild oats—it wouldn't be fair on her.'

The way his expression changed confirmed to her that

she had been right: a small child didn't fit into his game-plan—she would be an unwanted encumbrance, would cramp his style. Perhaps it was to his credit that he had such scruples; it was also fortunate, she reminded herself sternly—otherwise, married or not, she was quite sure he would regard her as fair game.

Saul drained his coffee—even though it must still have been very hot—and rose easily to his feet. 'I'll start with the attic, then.'

'I'll show you the way.' She would rather that he leave the house altogether, but at least he wouldn't be here in the kitchen with her, disturbing her equilibrium, making her feel as if she was coming down with some kind of fever.

'Oh, I think I can find it,' he responded with a sardonic smile. 'Straight up the stairs to the top, right?'

'Right.' Her own smile was as humourless as his. 'Mind you don't wake Emma.'

'I'll be careful.'

Left alone in the kitchen, Shelley sat for a few moments gazing absently at the empty mug he had just put down. It was one she had always rather liked; it had a pattern of butterflies on it, but she couldn't remember where she had bought it. . .

Why *had* she married Colin? she mused pensively. Because she had been lonely, because he had seemed to offer a security, a comfort that she had missed so terribly since Luke had died. And now this had happened. Didn't it give her the perfect excuse to escape from what she had begun to realise had been a very foolish mistake?

Or was that too easy? She had always believed that marriage vows were made to be kept, whether they were spoken in a register office or a church. It was supposed to be for better or worse, not something to be shrugged aside at the first hint of trouble—or the first hint that there might be greener grass on the other side of the fence. . .

Not that Saul Rainer represented greener grass, she reminded herself briskly—if she were to risk climbing over that particular fence, she was likely to find herself up to her neck in stinging nettles! And if he cared to waste his time searching the house for he-didn't-even-know-what that was up to him—she had some sewing to get on with.

It wasn't easy to concentrate, knowing he was in the house—Shelley kept pausing to listen to the small sounds of his moving about upstairs, of cupboards opening and closing, of his footfalls creaking on the floorboards. She knew when he went into her bedroom, visualised him walking round the big double bed and finding the book she was currently reading on her bedside table, *Madame Bovary*. How appropriate, she mused wryly—Flaubert's famously flawed heroine, fallen into adultery and finally taking her own life, might have lived in much earlier times, but she was still a vivid reminder of the danger of letting yourself be ruled by your emotions.

She heard him come downstairs and go into the front room; at least that was tidy—just wait till he went into the dining room! Lacking much need for it—they usually ate at the kitchen table—it had become the room in which Emma's larger toys were stored, as well as her buggy, and an airer festooned with damp clothes. Well, so what? No doubt he had a housekeeper and a couple of maids to clear up after him—this was real life.

Carefully she snipped off the trailing threads from the seam she had just sewn, and laid the little Paisley-print dress down on the table. There was just a bit of hand-stitching to do on it now—she could finish that tonight while she watched television. Packing away her sewing things, she closed up the sewing machine and carried it through into the dining room where it was stored along with the rest of the junk that needed to be close to hand but for which there was no proper home.

Saul followed her into the room, glancing around in wry humour. 'Your rumpus room?'

'We don't have a lot of dinner parties,' she returned lightly. 'I doubt if you'll find anything of Colin's in here.'

He shrugged. 'I might as well finish the job, now I've started. I never really had much hope—I just didn't want to leave any stone unturned.'

Shelley perched on the edge of the big old-fashioned walnut sideboard—given to her by an elderly aunt who had bestowed it with strict instructions that it must be properly looked after—and watched as he worked his way along the bookshelves on each side of the fireplace, pulling each book out one by one and fanning the pages to check that there was nothing folded between them, puffing out clouds of dust.

'Keep it up,' she remarked drily. 'You're doing a great job. I haven't dusted those shelves for years.'

'So I see,' he returned, slanting her a look of mild amusement. He picked up a photograph album and flicked it open; a loose snap fluttered to the floor, and he bent to pick it up, glancing at it with interest. 'Your first husband?' he enquired.

She nodded, moving across to take it from him, a small, wistful smile curving the corners of her soft mouth as she gazed at the picture. It had been taken just days before he had died, as he'd sat astride his big Harley Ultra Classic, an infant Emma propped on his lap as if she had been born to be a biker.

'He doesn't look much like Colin,' he remarked.

'Not much. . .' Over six feet tall and sturdily built, with a bristling black beard and wild hair, he looked like everyone's nightmare image of a biker. But he had been a gentle giant—you could see that in the way his big hands tenderly held his tiny daughter. It was so unfair that Emma would never know what a lovely man her daddy had been. . .

'It must have been very tough for you after he died,' Saul commented softly.

'It was.'

Slowly she became aware that she had let herself be captured by the spell of those dark, hypnotic eyes, held prisoner in their depths. Was this how he captured his prey, she wondered a little desperately—mesmerising them with that dark gaze, until they had no will of their own. . .?

He put up one hand, coiling his finger into a long tendril of her hair, drawing her slowly, inexorably towards him, until they were as close as that night when they had danced together. . . But now they were alone, and that evocative musky scent of maleness was drugging her mind, awakening some deep, instinctive response inside her that she was powerless to control.

She drew in her breath on a ragged sigh, her lips parting in helpless invitation as his head bent over hers. It wasn't fair—how could she possibly resist such wicked temptation? From the first time she had met him, she had been wondering what it would be like to kiss him, sometimes lying awake guiltily beside Colin as he slept, weaving magical fantasies that she had never thought could have a chance of coming true. And now he was here. . .

The fevered swirl of her blood was making her dizzy,

and she put up her hands against his wide chest to steady herself, feeling the supple resilience of hard muscle beneath the smooth, fine cotton of his shirt. His arms slid around her, curving her close against him, and then at long last his mouth brushed hers, lingered, tentatively tasting the sweetness within, his tongue sweeping languorously into the sensitive corners of her lips as she surrendered to the aching need inside her, reaching up on tiptoe to wrap her arms around his neck and hungrily kissing him back.

This was more, much more, than her imagination could have ever painted; there was something fierce in it, something almost primitive that both frightened and excited her. Her heart was drumming a racing rhythm, her body was responding on its own terms as she moved against him, and his tongue plundered deep into her mouth in a flagrantly sensual exploration, enflaming them both until the heat they were generating would have melted solid rock.

A whimpering cry from upstairs brought reality skidding back. With a small gasp of protest, as much at her own unforgivable behaviour as at his, she pushed herself away from him, her eyes reflecting the turmoil of her emotions as she lifted them to his. 'We. . .shouldn't have done that,' she choked out.

Saul smiled in wry affirmation. 'No, I don't suppose we should.'

'I'd. . .better go and see to Emma.'

She fled from the room, racing up the stairs, her cheeks hot with shame. How could she have let herself give in to temptation like that? She was married to Colin—whatever the reality of their relationship might have been. That one fact was inescapable.

By the time she reached the nursery, Emma was wide

awake, sitting up and chatting to Fred Bear in her own private language. She chuckled all the way through her nappy-change, jumbling along with the nursery rhymes Shelley sang to her, but when picked up to be carried down the stairs decided it was time to assert her independence. 'Down,' she insisted, wriggling.

'All right. Hold onto the rail and Mummy's hand, then,' Shelley conceded, patiently stepping down beside the tot as she plodded resolutely down each flight, her face furrowed with concentration. The last step was taken with a big jump, and then Emma was off and running to the kitchen, squealing with excitement about nothing at all.

Shelley cast a quick glance into the dining room as she passed; Saul wasn't there, and he wasn't in the kitchen either. Had he just gone, without even saying goodbye? But her disappointment was swiftly replaced by fury as she realised that the door to the cellar was open, and the light on down there.

Quickly she plucked Emma off her feet, swinging her up to her shoulder. 'Saul?' she called, a sharp edge in her voice.

He appeared at the foot of the steep steps, one dark eyebrow raised in polite enquiry.

She forced down her instinctive reaction, holding onto the reasons why she couldn't afford to let herself weaken again. 'I suppose it never occurred to you how dangerous it is to leave this door open?' she queried tersely. 'Emma could have fallen down.'

He looked momentarily surprised, and then shook his head in wry apology. 'No—I'm sorry, it *didn't* occur to me.' He started up the stairs towards her. 'I'm not used to having to think one jump ahead for a child of that age.'

She took a pace back as he came closer, preserving a

safe distance between them. 'Surely it's just plain common sense?'

'Probably,' he conceded, knowing as well as she did that her protest was almost as much a defence strategy as genuine annoyance. 'I'm sorry—it was thoughtless of me.' He closed the cellar door behind him. 'There.'

Shelley drew in a deep, steadying breath, and risked lifting her eyes to meet his. 'Did you find anything?'

'Nothing. He's eradicated himself very thoroughly indeed.' He smiled crookedly down at her. 'I'm sorry, but I suspect that probably means that he *was* planning this from the beginning.'

She shrugged at the implication, her feelings too mixed up to sort out. 'Oh, well, we'll see,' she murmured vaguely. 'What will you do now?'

'I'll leave it in the hands of my private investigator. Of course, it's quite possible that he's already left the country—probably on a false passport—in which case it could take quite a while to find him.'

She nodded. 'Well, if I hear anything else, I'll get in touch with you, of course,' she managed, struggling to deny the regret that was tugging at her heart. He would be going now, and she didn't know it she'd ever see him again. 'Er. . .goodbye, then.' She thrust out her hand, determined to end on a politely formal note.

He glanced down at her hand, smiling slowly in wry acknowledgement of the insurmountable barrier presented by the existence of the small child in her arms. 'Goodbye it is—under the circumstances,' he agreed, taking her hand and lifting it to place the lightest of kisses on the pulse that raced beneath the delicate skin inside her wrist. 'Pity—it could have been. . .very, very good.'

She watched him walk away, a hollow ache in her

heart. He climbed into his car, and the engine purred into life. Only as it pulled away from the kerb could she make herself close the front door, leaning back against it, staring up blankly at a small cobweb in the corner of the ceiling—she must have missed that yesterday when she had dusted. . .

Goodness, had that been only yesterday? In less than twenty-four hours her world had been turned inside out— the safe, secure world she had thought she had made for herself. And now, she acknowledged with an uncomfortable twinge of guilt, she knew that she hadn't really wanted that world at all.

How could she ever have fooled herself into believing that the kind of almost platonic relationship she had had with Colin could have satisfied her for long? She had told herself at the time that it was because she was still in love with Luke that she had felt only relieved that he had seemed to have little interest in the. . .intimate side of their marriage.

But it certainly wasn't that, she acknowledged wryly—there was absolutely nothing wrong with her physical responses. From the minute Saul Rainer had stepped into her life, she had been aware of a sizzling current running through her veins like electricity—while poor Colin, for all his commendable qualities, had never made her heartbeat accelerate for a single second.

She had tried so hard to convince herself that she had done the right thing, but deep in her heart she had always known that it couldn't work. Because there was one essential ingredient she had left out of the equation. Magic.

CHAPTER FOUR

'WELL, that was a very smart visitor you had yesterday. I saw the car pull up in the street, and I said to my George, "Who on earth can that be, coming down here with a car like that? He's taking a bit of a chance, parking it round here." Well, you know what some of the kids are like—see a car like that, and they'll be trying to break into it. . .'

'Yes, well. . .fortunately it was OK,' Shelley murmured with a thin smile. Mrs Timmins was the street gossip, and it could take half an hour to get away from her. Usually she was pretty adept at avoiding her, but this morning she had caught her on the corner as she was on her way back from the post office—Shelley wouldn't have put it past her to have been lying in wait for her behind Mr Patel's privet hedge.

'I know—I was keeping a bit of an eye on it for you, dear. Especially when I saw you go walking off down the road. "They can't have gone far," I said to George, "otherwise they'd have taken the car, and not left it there like that." I don't know what it's all coming to, I really don't, when you can't even park your car and—'

'Excuse me, Mrs Timmins,' Shelley cut in on her. 'There seems to be something happening outside my house—I'd better go and see.'

Mrs Timmins turned to look. 'Oh—they're putting a "For Sale" sign up. I never knew you was planning to move, dear. . .'

'I'm not!' She manoeuvred the buggy into line and

66

marched briskly down the pavement. 'Hey!' she called
out to the scruffily dressed man who was hammering a
wooden post into the ground just inside her front gate.
'What are you doing? You've got the wrong address.'

There was a red Mercedes parked by the kerb, and as
she drew level another man emerged from it, as sharply
immaculate as the other was scruffy. 'Number twenty-
seven, Linfield Road?' he queried. 'No—I don't think
we've got the wrong address.'

Shelley stared at him, bewildered. 'What do you mean?
This is *my* house—I live here, I own it, and I'm certainly
not planning to sell it.'

He smiled at her, rather in the way she imagined a
rattlesnake might smile. 'It's already been sold,' he
purred with sleek satisfaction. 'So you'd better see about
finding somewhere else to live, hadn't you? You
wouldn't want to be hanging about.'

The hint of menace in his tone was chilling, but she
wouldn't let herself be intimidated. She glared straight
back at him in frosty disdain. 'There's obviously been
some kind of misunderstanding,' she asserted forcefully.
'I told you—this house belongs to me, and it isn't
for sale.'

He shook his head, that snake-like smile still in place.
'Oh, there ain't no misunderstanding—not according to
the papers I've got here,' he responded, ostentatiously
consulting the clipboard in his hand. 'It's been bought by
me and my partners. Carry on, Baz,' he added, nodding to
his large companion.

'Stop, Baz!' Shelley countermanded the order without
hesitation. 'Show me the papers.'

His eyes—narrow eyes, too close together for him to
be trustworthy—glinted with malice; he didn't like being
defied—especially, she suspected, by a woman. He

handed her the clipboard, and with a last icy glare at him she glanced down at the sheaf of papers attached to it. The top one was a photocopy of a legal-looking document, granting Colin full power of attorney to act on her behalf. She read through it, stunned, to the bottom—and found herself looking at her own signature, duly sealed and witnessed.

'But. . .there's been some mistake. . .' she protested, feeling suddenly rather sick. 'I didn't sign this. At least. . .'

'Are you claiming the signature's a forgery?' the snake-man challenged belligerently.

'No. . .but. . .I did sign some forms a couple of weeks ago, but they were just to do with my tax returns. They weren't to sell the house.'

'Well, I'm sorry, baby—looks like you'd better sort it out with your husband. We bought the house legitimate, and paid him the money. So, if there's any stuff you want to take with you, you'd better get it packed up like a good girl—what gets left behind is ours.'

Shelley was still staring at the paper, but that 'baby' sparked her out of her shock. '*Don't* call me baby,' she snarled at him, her eyes flashing. 'And I am *not* packing my stuff. I don't know what's been going on, but my husband had no right to sell you the house—it belongs to me, not him. And I'm not moving.'

That chilling smile had turned to an even more unpleasant sneer. 'Now, that *would* be silly,' he advised, the implied threat unmistakable beneath his silky words. 'See, we want to sell the house—that's the business we're in. And we can't sell it with you in it, now, can we?'

'No, you can't.' A hard knot of panic was twisting her stomach, but she wasn't going to show him any fear.

'And you can't make me leave, either. At the very least you'd have to get a court order to evict me.'

He took a half-step towards her, and so did his large companion. 'Ah, we don't usually have to bother with those,' he purred. 'Do we, Baz? People usually change their minds about being obstinate, once they think about it. See, if we don't sell the house, Baz here don't get his wages, and that tends to upset him a bit—well, it's understandable, ain't it?'

Shelley had to draw in a long, steadying breath before she could be sure of having sufficient control over her voice. 'If you threaten me, I shall call the police,' she warned.

He merely laughed. 'But the police can't be here all the time, can they?' he taunted. 'Now, why don't you be sensible? We wouldn't want anything. . .unfortunate to happen, would we? Not to you and your little girl. That would be *such* a pity.'

He reached out one hand to stroke Emma's blonde hair, but Shelley jerked the buggy quickly away. 'Don't you dare touch her!' she spat at him, tears rising to choke her. 'Just go away—and take this with you!' With a last show of courage, she snatched up the 'For Sale' board and threw it down on the pavement, and then marched up the path to the front door, fumbling frantically with her keys to let herself in.

Behind her came the sound of mocking laughter. 'All right, Mrs Clarke—we'll give you until tomorrow morning. But no longer than that, mind. I'm afraid Baz ain't a very patient sort of person.'

She slammed the door in his face.

But her bravado ebbed quickly away, and she had to sit down on the bottom of the stairs as her legs almost collapsed beneath her. Emma, still in her buggy, was gazing at her with wide blue eyes, as if sensing that something was wrong but not sure what it was.

'What are we going to do, Emmy?' she whispered raggedly. 'Those horrid men are saying Daddy-Colin's sold them our house. I can't believe he'd do that to us.' The tears spilled over and began to stream down her face. 'This is our *home*. If I let them turn us out, we don't have anywhere to go.'

There could be no doubt now that Saul Rainer was telling the truth, she acknowledged bitterly—Colin had cheated both of them. Oh, he had been clever. If anyone else had asked her to sign anything, she would have examined it thoroughly first, but she had trusted Colin— after all, he was her husband. So when he had offered to deal with all her tax affairs for her she had been more than happy to let him.

And he had picked his time well. The night he had given her the papers to sign she had been tired—Emma had been grizzling with her teeth all day. She had simply scrawled her signature in the places he had indicated, barely listening to his somewhat pedantic explanations of the small print. He must have slipped the attorney document in among the others, and she hadn't even noticed.

The realisation that he had deliberately targeted her, that he had married her while planning to steal the very roof from over her head made her feel almost physically sick. But what was she going to do? That was her signature on the papers—even if she went to the police, would she be able to prove that he had tricked her, and get her house back? And in the meantime the threats those men had made had to be taken seriously.

Guided by an instinct she hadn't even been aware of,

she found herself reaching for the telephone and dialling the number on the card tucked beneath it.

'Mr Rainer's office,' a crisp, businesslike voice announced.

'Oh. . .er. . .is Mr Rainer there, please?' she stammered awkwardly.

'He's in a meeting at the moment. Can I take a message?'

'A meeting?' Shelley repeated, half-dazed. 'How long will he be?'

'I'm afraid it's difficult to say,' came the cool response. 'He should be free by lunchtime. Shall I ask him to call you back?'

'Yes. . .er. . .no, I. . . It doesn't matter. Thank you.' Talking to him on the telephone would be no good any-way—she needed to see him. Glancing at her watch, she calculated swiftly that if she was lucky with the buses she could be at his office by lunchtime. Scuffing the back of her hand across her eyes to wipe away the tears, she seized the buggy and swung her bag onto her shoulder and headed out of the front door.

It started to rain heavily as the bus crossed the wide span of Waterloo Bridge; the bus was full, and Emma was getting fractious. Struggling to get off the bus with the protesting child under one arm and her bag over her shoulder, dragging the awkward buggy with her, Shelley had cause to reflect ruefully on the indifference of the great British public, not one of whom offered to help.

By the time they reached the elegant glass-fronted entrance of Rainer House, tucked round behind New Oxford Street, Emma was screaming at the top of her lungs, her face scarlet with rage, and Shelley was very close to being at the end of her tether—and in no mood for any argument with the two glossy-lipped receptionists behind their fern-decked counter. Fortunately one was on the telephone and the other engaged with another visitor as Shelley manoeuvred her way awkwardly through the revolving door, giving her the opportunity to slip straight past and duck into a lift that had just finished disgorging its passengers—ignoring a sharp call of, 'Madam? Can I help you?'

She pressed the button for the top floor, leaning back against the wall and closing her eyes, breathing deeply to try to steady her shredded nerves. It had been such a hassle simply getting here that she hadn't really stopped to question the automatic impulse to seek Saul's help, but now the doubts were beginning to flood in. Maybe he wouldn't welcome the imposition of her problems. . . But she was here now—at least she might as well see him.

She had only a rough idea of the layout of the top floor—Colin had taken her on a brief conducted tour shortly after they had got married. But it was probably pretty similar to the layout of his own floor, several rungs down, and she had been there two or three times. Stepping out of the lift, she set off down the passage at a brisk pace, trying to look as if she had every right to be there, just in case anyone should challenge her—not an easy act to pass off with Emma at peak decibels, hammering her heels furiously against the footrest of the buggy.

The door was the last one at the end of the passage—and not designed for getting a buggy-load of protesting toddler through with aplomb. Her dignity wasn't helped by getting the strap of her bag hooked on the doorhandle either, almost tipping her over backwards as the door swung shut behind her. She really couldn't blame the

immaculately groomed creature behind the desk for looking at her in blank astonishment—she was as much out
of place in these smart, businesslike surroundings as Saul
had been in her cluttered kitchen.

'Can I help you?' came the automatic query, the frigid
politeness of the tone failing to mask a very refined
distaste for someone so evidently out of control of every
aspect of her life.

'I. . .need to see Sau. . .Mr Rainer,' Shelley managed,
her voice ragged with agitation.

'I'm afraid he can't be disturbed at present.'

Since Emma at least had no respect for the niceties of
business etiquette, and was intent on disturbing anyone
within a five-mile radius, it was really not surprising that
the far door opened abruptly and Saul himself appeared,
a startled expression on his face. 'What the. . .? Shelley?
Whatever's the matter?'

Shelley took one look at him, and did exactly what
she had been promising herself she wouldn't do: she
burst into tears.

In two strides he was across the room, wrapping his
arms around her. Shaken by sobs that she couldn't control, she let herself lean against him, clinging to the front
of his immaculate jacket, past caring what his secretary
or anyone else thought. She knew she shouldn't let herself give in to this treacherous temptation to depend on
his strength, but she had none left of her own.

He was holding her tight, stroking his hand over her
hair the way she stroked Emma's when she was soothing
her to sleep. 'What's the matter? What's happened?'
he asked.

'He's sold my house,' she managed brokenly. 'Two
men came this morning to put up a "For Sale" sign. I
knew nothing about it—he tricked me into signing the

papers. They. . . They were threatening me that if I don't get out by tomorrow. . . I'm sorry—I shouldn't have bothered you, but I didn't know what else to do.'

'That's OK,' Saul assured her gently. 'I'm glad you came to me. Cathy, make my apologies and adjourn the meeting until tomorrow, would you?' he added to his secretary. 'And then bring us coffee.'

Shelley struggled to swallow her tears. 'I'm sorry,' she mumbled on a hiccup. 'I didn't mean to interrupt you.'

He laughed with dry humour, giving her his handkerchief. 'You arrived at a very opportune moment,' he remarked. 'It was a very dull meeting with some very dull planning officials, and I needed an excuse to break off at that point. Now, come into my office and tell me exactly what's happened.'

She dabbed her eyes, stepping back awkwardly out of the circle of his arms. 'Thank you. I. . .think I need to see to Emma first, though.' She smiled up at him a little crookedly. 'She probably needs to have her nappy changed.'

He slanted a wry glance down at the red-faced child, who seemed to have temporarily exhausted herself with screaming—though she looked as if she was keying herself up for a further bout. 'In that case, you can use my washroom,' he offered. 'I assume you've got the necessary. . .er. . .whatever.'

'Of course,' she assured him, amused in spite of everything by his ignorance of the needs of small children. 'I won't be long.'

His secretary, who had just finished ushering the greysuited men whom Saul had been seeing out of the other door, swept a cool glance over Shelley as she wheeled the buggy into his office and bent to unfasten the straps, lifting Emma into her arms. She was clearly much too

professional to question this bizarre invasion, but she had
her own subtle way of conveying her opinion—that one
look spoke volumes.

Shelley simply ignored her—she had too many other
things on her mind to worry about Saul's secretary.
'Come on, chick, let's get you sorted,' she cooed to the
fractious Emma. 'You'll feel much better when you've
got a nice clean nappy on.'

It would give her a few essential minutes to recover her
own composure too, she reflected, retreating thankfully
through the door that Saul was holding open. It had
probably been a stupid idea to come here—it was
unlikely that he would be able to do anything to help,
and she was just making a nuisance of herself.

The washroom was huge and very luxurious—pale
grey marble lined the walls and floor, and you could have
held a party in the shower cubicle. A timely reminder, she
mused wryly; when they talked about how the other half
lived, this was the other half they meant. This room, this
office suite, this whole building belonged to Saul Rainer,
along with all the popular stores that bore his name—
and there was probably plenty more that she didn't even
know about. Even the cool half-million Colin had pur-
loined would be little more than a drop in the ocean to
him. That kind of wealth created a gulf between them
that was too wide to bridge—and it would be wise not
to let herself forget that.

Once Emma was restored to her usual sweet, happy
self, Shelley quickly rinsed her own face in cool water,
drying it on one of the fluffy white towels stacked on a
shelf beside the basin. Studying herself wryly in the
mirror, she was forced to admit that she wasn't looking
her best—her eyes were rimmed with pink, and several

wayward strands of hair had slid from the band that tied
it up on top of her head.

Not that it mattered, she chided herself sharply; all
that was necessary was that she presented a reasonably
tidy face to the world. It wasn't as if she was trying to
impress anyone—that wasn't why she was here. Quickly
she loosened her hair and dragged her hairbrush through
it, and tied it up again, and then slicked her lips with a
touch of clear gloss. The improvement was only slight,
but it made her feel a little better.

Emma was investigating the bidet with scientific curiosity. 'Come on, then—outside,' Shelley coaxed. 'How
about some of your orange juice? Would you like that?'

'Oran' joos,' Emma nodded eagerly, launching herself
in a stomping run across Saul's office as Shelley opened
the door. In the middle of the floor she stopped, swaying
slightly as she gazed around at the unfamiliar location,
and then she caught sight of Saul, and smiled a little
uncertainly, looking back at her mother to check that
everything was OK.

'It's all right, chick—that's Uncle Saul,' Shelley
assured her gently.

He arched one dark eyebrow in quizzical amusement
at being thus arbitrarily dragged into the family. 'She's
looking a little happier now than she was a few minutes
ago, anyway,' he remarked with a touch of wry humour.
'Would she like a drink of milk or something? Can she
use a cup?'

'It's OK; I've got her juice here,' Shelley responded,
taking Emma's travelling cup from her bag and deftly
clicking up the spout. 'Here you are, chickadee—say
thank you.'

'T'ank you,' the child parroted obediently, gazing up

wide-eyed at the tall man beside her as she took the cup in both hands and tipped it up to her mouth.

Saul smiled crookedly. 'I wondered what you kept in there. Everything but the kitchen sink, apparently.'

'Oh, I think I've probably got one of those in here somewhere,' she returned on a note of humour. 'It's the first motto of motherhood—Be prepared for anything!'

The joke fell a little flat; he was beginning to tolerate Emma's presence—even, it sometimes seemed, to enjoy it—but any mention of the responsibilities that went with the pleasure a small child could bring was still apparently taboo.

He moved over to a grouping of comfortable armchairs, softly upholstered in pale grey hide, around a large coffee-table made from a single slab of polished marble, inviting her to join him. No expense spared here either, she reflected as she glanced around the spacious room properly for the first time.

It might have been a slight exaggeration to say that it was the size of a football pitch, but it had a light, airy feel about it that made it seem vast, with a pale grey carpet, and soft grey walls hung with a few striking modern paintings—was that a *real* Jackson Pollock behind his desk?—to add vivid splashes of colour. And the view along the sweeping curve of Shaftesbury Avenue was quite something as well.

'The coffee will be here in a moment,' he said. 'You must be feeling pretty shaken.'

She nodded, slanting him a wry smile. 'I didn't know what to do—that's why I. . .came to see you.' The original blind panic had faded a little, leaving her with a feeling of bleak emptiness. 'I can't believe Colin could do a thing like that. I just keep wondering how I could have been such a fool. Why didn't I see through him? I never thought I was such a lousy judge of character.'

'You and me both, I'm afraid,' he responded drily. 'He appears to be quite an expert conman. It seems there can be little doubt now that it was all deliberately planned from the very beginning.'

'No, I suppose not,' she conceded. She could no longer deny it; nor could she deny the secret tinge of relief at knowing that it wasn't Saul who had stolen the money to cheat his own shareholders. 'Have you heard anything from your private investigator?' she enquired to take her mind away from that train of thought.

He shook his head. 'Not yet. They're checking out the information from New Zealand, as well as trying to find out anything more about what he's been up to since he came over here. It could be quite useful for you to meet with them some time.'

'Of course. . . Emma, what is it you want? No, put your cup down first. I think she wants your keys again,' she added to Saul with a wry smile.

'Is that so?' He smiled down at the toddler clinging to his knee, and pulled his keys from his pocket, dangling them for her. 'Here you are.'

She took them from him, looked at them in deep concentration, and then handed them back. He looked a little surprised, and went to put them back in his pocket, but the child protested loudly, holding out her hand. Shelley laughed. 'You're supposed to give them to her again,' she explained. 'It's a game.'

'Ah, I see.' He slapped the keys down lightly into the podgy, outstretched hand, and Emma giggled in delight, slapping them back into his. The exchange was repeated, as Shelley watched in surprise—she would never have expected Saul Rainer to be so patient with the little girl. 'You little monkey,' he teased, laughing as he reached down to tickle the child's chubby tummy. 'You'd have me doing this all day, wouldn't you?'

At that moment there was a tap on the door, and his secretary appeared, carrying a silver tray with the coffee things. She raised one finely arched eyebrow in well-bred astonishment at the sight of Emma, who was trying to clamber up onto Saul's knee, and the look she slanted towards Shelley now conveyed open hostility.

'Really, Saul—baby-sitting?' she queried on a note of sophisticated teasing that set Shelley's teeth on edge. 'I never thought I'd see the day!'

'Here—I'll take her,' Shelley offered quickly, reaching over to lift her daughter onto her own lap. 'Come on, Emma, there's a good girl.' To her relief, the toddler didn't make a fuss. After her earlier screaming bout, she was tired enough to settle, her cheek resting on her chubby hand, and fell asleep almost at once.

Saul glanced up at his secretary, smiling—if he was embarrassed at being caught acting so out of character he gave no sign of it. 'Ah, the coffee. Thank you, Cathy—just put it on the table, would you? By the way, have you met Shelley before? Colin's wife. She was at the company party.'

'I think we spoke briefly.' Shelley found a slim, manicured hand being held out to her. 'How do you do, Shelley? What a pretty name—short for Michelle, I take it?'

'No, it's just Shelley,' she responded blandly, accepting the proffered handshake.

The secretary's smile was the thinnest veneer of politeness. 'So, you're Colin's wife,' she remarked in a tone that eloquently conveyed her opinion of anyone dim enough to marry a crooked accountant. 'Do you have any idea where he is?'

'No, I'm afraid I don't,' Shelley responded, struggling to hold onto what was left of her dignity; if she was honest, she was rather inclined to agree with the other woman's assessment of her situation. 'I haven't seen him for two days.'

'Oh. What a pity. . . Saul, the evaluation report on the TFT resistors has arrived, and I've had the quotes for the Tokyo exhibition—do you want me to go ahead and book it?'

'Yes, please, Cathy. You'll be able to come with me that week?'

'Of course.'

The smile was that of the cat who had got the cream, and Shelley felt a stab of something she didn't care to examine too closely. Was he having an affair with his secretary? She was certainly the sort she would imagine he would go for—chic and immaculately groomed in tailored grey, with an air of effortless self-assurance and the pure vowels that were unmistakably the product of an expensive private education.

Dammit, she was *jealous*! It wasn't an emotion she had ever felt before—Luke had never given her any reason to feel jealous, and Colin. . . Well, to be honest, she couldn't imagine it. But she knew that was what it was—and she didn't like the way it made her feel.

Saul was pouring the coffee—from a silver Georgian coffee-pot, Shelley noted, that matched the cream jug and sugar bowl. 'Cream and sugar?' he enquired.

'Just a dash of cream, thank you,' she managed to respond.

He handed her the cup, and then leaned back in his seat, regarding her across the low table with that steady dark gaze. 'So, tell me exactly what happened,' he said. 'How did Colin trick you into signing the papers?'

She smiled wryly. It was a little embarrassing to have to admit how stupid she had been, but she told him the whole story, and he listened intently, occasionally putting in a question to clarify the details.

'There was no mortgage?'

Shelley shook her head. 'No. Luke's life insurance had paid it off.'

'Who are the people who've bought it?'

'It's some sort of property investment company—they're just planning to sell it on again.'

'Ah!' She slanted him a questioning look, and he went on to explain. 'Unfortunately there are a few of those kinds of shady companies around. They operate on the fringes of the law, buying up properties that are going cheap for some reason—usually because there's a sitting tenant, or because the owner's desperate for a quick sale. Then they harass anyone who's living there into leaving, and put the place back on the market as quickly as possible to make a nice little profit.'

Shelley pulled a wry face. 'Do you think there's anything I can do?' she asked in bleak tones.

The grim set of his mouth gave her little cause for optimism. 'I take it you *did* sign the papers?' he queried. 'The signature wasn't a forgery?'

'Well, if it was it was a damned good one,' Shelley responded with a trace of bitter humour. 'It certainly looked like my signature, even to me.'

'Was it countersigned by witnesses?'

'The paper I signed wasn't, but the one that man had was. They must have signed it afterwards. . . That would make it invalid, wouldn't it?' she added, grasping at the one shred of hope she could see.

'Technically,' he agreed, though his tone eloquently

conveyed his doubt. 'Of course, the difficulty would be proving it.'

'But surely it would have needed a solicitor to deal with something as important as that?' she protested.

'True. Unfortunately there are a few shady solicitors around too, who could be persuaded to sell out their professional ethics for a nice thick slice of the action. The first thing to do would be to get hold of a copy of the papers.'

'But in court it would still be my word against theirs, wouldn't it?' she mused bleakly. 'There would be no guarantee that I could prove they'd acted improperly.'

'I'm afraid not,' he acknowledged with a grim smile. He picked up the coffee-jug, offering her a second cup. 'Those papers—did they relate only to the house?'

She glanced across at him, startled by the question. 'What do you mean?'

'Well, for example, what about the compensation you received for Luke's accident? The insurance?'

'I haven't had the compensation yet,' she responded, her voice a little unsteady. 'It takes ages—they have to wait for the other driver to be prosecuted, and then for his appeal to go through, and then his insurance company argues over how much they're going to pay out. But there was Luke's life insurance, and the money from the sale of the shop—that's what I've been living on. . .' Her cheeks had gone pale. 'You don't think he's touched that as well, do you?'

'I think you'd better check.'

It took just a couple of telephone calls to confirm the worst. Colin had transferred most of the money out of her deposit account, and had cashed in her unit trusts two days ago—the day he had disappeared. He had left her with just a few hundred pounds in her current account.

She sat hugging the sleeping child on her lap, tears stinging her eyes. 'Damn him!' she breathed. 'Damn him! I wish I'd never set eyes on him. He's cheated me, and he's stolen Emma's future—I'll never forgive him for that.'

Saul had gone across to a small drinks cabinet in the corner, and returned with a glass of brandy. 'Here—I think you need something a little stronger than coffee.'

She glanced up at him with eyes still dark from shock. 'But I don't drink. . .'

'Purely medicinal,' he insisted, putting the glass into her hand and guiding it to her lips. 'Drink it.'

She drank it back it one gulp, the fiery liquid scalding her throat. 'I suppose it's a good job the compensation hadn't come through,' she mused, struggling to find a trace of silver lining in the mass of dark clouds crowding over her. 'He'd have had that as well.'

'I suspect that may have been what he was after,' he surmised drily. 'Could he have seen anything about it in the papers?'

'It was in the local paper when the trial was on. The driver who hit Luke was on the local council, and he pleaded not guilty; there was quite a big fuss about it. They used a photo of me and Emma on the front page the day the verdict was announced—but that was months before I met Colin.'

'He could have been planning it for that long.' He frowned. 'I'm sorry, but I suspect he may have done this kind of thing before—it's too complicated a scam to have been the first time.'

'You mean. . .you think he could be a professional conman?'

'I'm afraid it looks that way. I don't suppose it's any consolation, but I suspect you may well have been his primary target from the beginning. In fact, his job here could have been the camouflage, creating the right aura of respectability to impress you, rather than the other way round as I first thought.'

'But then why did he steal from you as well?' she argued. 'Surely that would just double the risk of getting caught?'

'Greed. . .over-confidence. . . If he's got away with it a few times in the past, he could have started to believe he was too clever. But this time he could find he's bitten off rather more than he can chew,' he added, his voice quiet but all the more menacing for that. 'The police might not have the resources to pursue him, but I do. And I'll find him.'

Shelley felt a small, cold shiver run down her spine; she could almost feel sorry for Colin. But Saul's grim determination was the only chance she had of getting any of her own money back. She brushed a hand over her eyes, and it came away wet with tears. 'I still find it hard to believe,' she mused. 'He seemed so. . .well, nice.'

'That's his stock-in-trade, I'm afraid,' Saul responded drily. 'He has to be plausible, convincing—smiling while he's robbing you blind. But, for the moment, you have to consider what you're going to do. You can't go back to your own house—those men will be back tomorrow.'

'I know. I suppose I could get an injunction, but I doubt if that would do a lot of good against people like that.' She sighed, glancing down at her small daughter sleeping peacefully in her buggy, one rosy cheek resting on one plump little hand. 'I hate to just give in to them. If it was just me, I'd stand my ground and refuse to budge, but. . .'

Saul shook his head firmly. 'No—it's too dangerous. Is there anywhere else you can stay for the time being?'

'Well, there's my father and stepmother,' she mused in doubtful tones. 'If I knew how long it might be for. . .'

'It's hard to say, but it's likely to be some time,' he advised, his voice serious. 'Look, I have a house in Sussex, near Chichester—you'd be welcome to stay down there for a while.'

'Oh but. . .I couldn't,' she protested, feeling her cheeks flame a heated red. 'I wouldn't want to. . .impose on you. . .'

'You wouldn't be.' His smile was grim. 'I feel a certain responsibility for what's happened—if my personnel people had done their job properly, we might have caught him out before he had a chance to do you any harm.'

Shelley hesitated. It was tempting—too tempting. Particularly when her only alternative was the sofa in her stepmother's intimidatingly tidy sitting room. . .

'I shan't be there,' he added with a faint smile, shrewdly guessing the cause of her uncertainty. 'I rarely get the chance to spend much time there. There's just my mother's old housekeeper, who stayed on to keep an eye on the place for me; she should have retired, but she's been there for ever and she doesn't really have anywhere else to go. And Emma will like it—the garden runs right down to the sea.'

'Well. . .' She knew she shouldn't; she would be in his debt, and that was not a place she wanted to be. But she didn't believe he would be the sort to take advantage of that. And besides, he wouldn't actually be there himself. There was really no good reason to turn down such a helpful invitation. 'All right,' she conceded with an unsteady smile. 'Thank you very much—it's very kind of you.'

'Good.' He nodded, and rose to his feet, moving briskly over to his desk to pick up the phone. 'I'll arrange for one of my staff to take you home to pack whatever you need—I suggest you bring any valuables with you as well. I'll drive you down there myself later this afternoon. In the meantime, I'll have a couple of security men put in your house to make sure there's no trouble.'

Shelley nodded weakly. Under normal circumstances, she would have objected most forcefully to being taken over in such a high-handed manner. But these were not normal circumstances, and it was just such a relief to have someone to lean on, someone to fight the dragons for her. She wasn't going to argue with him.

CHAPTER FIVE

THE spring sunshine was bright on the water, but the stiff breeze was a reminder that it was still only late March. Out in the bay a white-sailed yacht was skimming across the waves, while overhead the trill of a curlew and the raucous chatter of seagulls filled the air.

This little corner of the waterfront—you couldn't really call it a beach—was quite private. Tucked into one of the many sheltered inlets of Chichester Harbour, it was safe from the rough storms that could sometimes blow up in the Solent. There wasn't really any sand—just a kind of muddy ooze—but there was a wooden jetty which provided a convenient place to sit, and the rock pools were an endless source of entertainment for Emma.

They had been here for a little over a week now, and Shelley was glad that she had come. Here in these tranquil surroundings, she had been able to forget her worries for a while, and relax. Her only fear was that she was coming to love the beautiful house with its tree-shaded garden leading down to the sea a little too much.

It stood on a low rise of ground, skimmed by the coast road which here sheered inland for a short distance. Built in the nineteen-twenties by Saul's great-uncle Stanford, who had spent most of his life in the Far East, it was of gracious proportions, with white stuccoed walls and a steep-pitched slate roof, and a wide brick terrace at the back.

Every room was filled with the treasures he had

brought home—dark, carved furniture, some of it exquis-
itely inlaid, as well as ornaments of jade and ivory, and
dozens of sepia-tinted photographs of Edwardian soldiers
and ladies, and dark-skinned Javanese in their traditional
loose white robes.

The effect could all too easily been heavy and ugly, but
the height of the rooms, with their tall, wide, south-facing
windows invited the sunlight in, and the walls had been
papered in a pale peach colour that brought out the
warmth of the rich dark wood. Saul had told her that it
had been inherited first by his mother, and it was she
who had been responsible for its uncontrived elegance—
though since she had died some five years ago he'd rarely
visited.

Shelley had felt rather awkward at first, afraid Emma
would break something or spill something on one of the
carpets. But the welcome they were given by Winnie,
the elderly housekeeper, had quickly reassured her. 'Oh,
don't you go worrying! She's a little angel. Besides, what
are a few old ornaments? It's so nice to have a child
around the place—and I'm quite sure Miss Rosemary
would have said the same.'

It was clear that the housekeeper had been devoted to
Saul's mother, and, looking at the photographs of her
that were dotted around all over the place, Shelley felt
she would have liked her too. Not particularly a beauty,
she had had her son's strong bone structure, and a look
of kindly common sense that shone through her warm
smile. And someone who could create such a charming
home must have been a special sort of person.

Shelley stood and filled her lungs with the crisp, salt-
tanged air. She and Emma were both huddled in sweaters
over their shorts, plastic sandals on their feet as they
splashed among the shallow rock-pools. 'Look, Emma—

see the shrimps?' She pointed to the tiny grey-brown creatures almost invisible against the muddy ooze at the bottom of the pool. 'Quickly, bring the net.'

'Caught anything?'

Startled, she swivelled her head to squint up at the man who had appeared on the wooden jetty above them, his silhouette tall and broad against the afternoon sun. She hadn't been expecting to see Saul Rainer again so soon—he hadn't said that he would be coming down. 'What are you doing here?' she demanded, a little short of breath.

He laughed in lazy humour. 'I live here, remember?' he countered, jumping lightly down from the jetty onto the flat rocks beneath and coming over to crouch beside her.

Shelley could feel a slight blush of pink creeping into her cheeks. For the past week she had been telling herself that her imagination was painting his image larger than life, but now that he was here. . . 'You said you probably wouldn't be down again for a while,' she returned, pleased that in spite of the wild acceleration of her heartbeat she could still manage to keep her voice commendably even.

'It's Easter this weekend,' he reminded her, a glint of amusement in his dark eyes. 'Even I take a break sometimes.'

'Of course. I didn't mean. . . I'm sorry. . .' Dammit, why did she have to get so flustered when he looked at her like that?

'There's nothing for you to be sorry about,' he returned on a note of taunting mockery, his appreciative gaze skimming over her short shorts and the long, lissom legs beneath, as if to suggest that the sight of them was compensation enough for any inconvenience her presence might cause.

At that moment Emma, who had been deep in concentration with her net in the shallows of the pool, gave a squeal of delight and swept the net high into the air, showering both adults with sea-water.

'Clever girl!' Shelley cried, glad of the distraction. 'What have you caught?'

'Shrimp!' she lisped in triumph, poking the net with its dripping cargo of seaweed and wriggling shrimps towards them, forcing them both into a swift retreat to avoid a second soaking.

'Put them in the bucket, then,' Shelley instructed her gently, helping to tip the precious catch into the yellow plastic bucket, from where they would be discreetly returned to the pool in due course.

'It's a pity the beach isn't better here—you could build sand castles,' Saul remarked, glancing round at the muddy flats exposed by the low tide.

'Oh, we've been enjoying ourselves well enough, playing in the rock pools,' Shelley returned brightly. 'Haven't we, chick?'

'Have you been into Portsmouth?' he asked. 'You can visit the *Victory*, and go aboard a submarine, and there's a marine aquarium that I'm sure she'd love.'

'No, we haven't,' Shelley responded, a little surprised that he should take such an interest in Emma's entertainment. 'I know you said I could borrow your car, but. . .I wasn't sure about driving it in a strange town. Besides, it hasn't got a child-seat,' she added with a crooked smile—hers was in the back of Colin's car, and heaven only knew where that was now.

That thought brought her back to an uncomfortable recollection of why she was here—and why she shouldn't be letting herself be so aware of this man beside her. She rose a little awkwardly to her feet—but that only made it worse as he stood up too, so tall, so uncompromisingly male, making her mouth feel suddenly dry.

She had only ever seen him in a suit and wearing a tie, but now he had taken off his jacket and discarded the tie, leaving his collar loose—and within its shadow she could just glimpse the smattering of rough dark male hair that curled at the base of his throat. . . Her own throat constricted as she tried to mask her refusal to look up at him by bending to pick up Emma's bucket and spade.

'Come on then, chick,' she said, holding out her hand to the little girl. 'Shall we go and see what Auntie Winnie's got for your tea?'

Saul fell into step beside her as they climbed the steps and strolled up through the garden. 'I heard from my investigators this morning,' he told her, his voice cool and flat. 'They've tracked down what's happened to some of your money.'

'Oh?' She glanced up at him in startled question. For the past week she had been racking her brains, trying to think of some alternative explanation for what had happened, some way that it could all have been a mistake or a misunderstanding—though she had been forced to admit that it seemed highly unlikely. 'How did they manage to find it?'

He shrugged those wide shoulders, the hard muscles moving smoothly beneath his crisp white shirt. 'I don't question their methods—so long as they get results. It appears that Colin has been trying to cover his tracks by putting the money through half-a-dozen different bank accounts. But now they've got a fix on him; the minute he tries to touch any of it, we'll know.'

Shelley felt again that small shiver of chill at the note of grim ruthlessness in his voice. When Colin was found there was going to be one hell of a confrontation. 'So we just have to wait?' she asked a little unsteadily.

'We just have to wait. But in the meantime. . .' He slanted her a slightly crooked smile that made her heart flip over. 'It's the sponsors' pre-season party for the race team on Saturday evening. I thought you might like to come.'

She glanced up at him, shocked. 'A party for the race team? But. . .I mean, I'm not sure that I should—under the circumstances.'

'What circumstances?' he countered obdurately. 'You've done nothing wrong—you're not responsible for your husband's criminal activities. What were you planning to do? Hide away for the rest of your life? Don't be silly.'

'I'm not being silly,' she protested, stung. 'It's just. . .I *am* still married, and. . .'

Those dark eyes glinted with sardonic humour. 'Don't you think, after what he's done, your marriage is as good as over?' he queried drily.

'I suppose. . . But. . .' But, in spite of everything, she didn't want to think about that just yet; she had never expected that she would ever find herself in the divorce court. And besides, without the barrier of her marriage between them, she was afraid it would be even more difficult to keep him at arm's length. And she was afraid of the consequences of letting herself be lured into having an affair with him; it was a risk she couldn't afford to take.

'I'm not talking about a romantic candlelit dinner for two,' he assured her, too perceptive not to know her fears. 'There'll be about a hundred people there. You'll enjoy it.'

She hesitated, struggling against the temptation. 'What about Emma?' she argued weakly. 'It. . .doesn't sound like the sort of thing you can drag a toddler along to.'

'I'm sure Winnie will be delighted to babysit for you.'

Shelley was quite sure that she would. Oh, dammit, why did it have to be so hard to do the right thing? 'All right,' she conceded, giving up the unequal struggle. 'Thank you for inviting me.'

'Thank you for accepting,' he responded, very formal, but the glint in those dark eyes warned her to be wary— she must give him no reason to believe that she was agreeing to anything more.

'Repeat after me—I am a married woman, and I am not going to have an affair with Saul Rainer.' The words were resolute enough, but the green eyes gazing back at her from the mirror held a guilty uncertainty. She was much too vulnerable to him—and unfortunately he knew it.

Perhaps if her marriage to Colin had been a little more. . .successful in that respect she would have been better able to keep things in perspective. But his apparent lack of interest in that side of their relationship had slowly undermined her confidence, made her begin to doubt her own attractiveness.

She hadn't really thought much of it, at first—in fact it had seemed rather sweet when he had said that he wanted to wait until their wedding night. But even then. . .well. . .they hadn't exactly set the bed-sheets alight. As the days—and nights—had passed, she had begun to wonder whether it was her fault. Maybe she was too tall, too skinny . . . Oh, Luke had been crazy about her, but then maybe Luke had been odd—heaven only knew, most people would have been quick enough to say that he was. So to have a man like Saul Rainer take an interest in her had been a heady experience—heady and dangerous.

But try as she might to rationalise it, there was an ache inside her that wouldn't go away, and she knew that there was only one cure for it. 'Are you stupid?' she demanded of the wistful reflection in the mirror. 'The last thing you want to do is go to bed with him. You'd be just one more conquest to add to his score.'

Why hadn't he warned her that he was planning to come down for the Easter weekend? He had deliberately given her to understand that he rarely visited the house. If she had known that he would be here she might have thought more than twice about accepting his invitation. At least, she liked to think that she would.

And he had certainly put himself out to be amenable, offering to take her and Emma into Portsmouth to visit the attractions that had been set up for tourists, even seeming quite happy to carry Emma around on his shoulders for most of the afternoon. And he really had tried to be patient with her—even when she had thrown a minor tantrum in the submarine museum because she didn't want to be dragged away from one of the brightly lit exhibits, or when she had pleaded for an ice cream, only to let it melt all down the front of her dungarees.

Was she being cynical to wonder if he had an ulterior motive for being so friendly? A short while ago she would never even have thought of that, she mused wryly, but now. . .she no longer had much faith in her own judgement. Not that it made any material difference; a day of playing at being 'Uncle Saul' was one thing—it was something else to take on another man's child as a long-term commitment. And only that would be good enough.

With a small sigh she shook her head and turned away from the mirror. She was seriously beginning to doubt the wisdom of agreeing to go to this thing this evening— it was his world, and it would only highlight the fact that she didn't belong in it. She had seen on television the type of women who hung around the motor-racing scene—all blonde highlights and toothpaste smiles, and clothes cut to show off the maximum amount of sunbed tan.

Almost in defiance, she had stuck to her customary black, with a dress she had made herself, in fact—in a plain, satin-type fabric, simple and sleeveless, and tailored to fit her slim figure. And with her only jewellery being a pair of her wildest earrings and her hair tumbling down her back in a riot of russet curls she had no doubt that she would look very much out of place.

But she had never cared what people thought of her; she always dressed to please herself, and she had no intention of changing that habit now. Resolutely squaring her shoulders, she picked up her handbag and pulled open the door—almost colliding with Saul as she stepped out into the passage.

Her heart gave a sharp thud. He had changed the casual clothes he had been wearing earlier for a formal dinner jacket, with a crisply pin-tucked white shirt and a dark blue silk bow-tie. The jacket was beautifully cut, moulding elegantly over those wide shoulders, but he wore it with the kind of suave ease that subtly underlined the hint of raw male magnetism that he seemed to exude without any conscious effort.

'Ah, there you are,' he greeted her with a lazy smile. Those dark eyes slid down over her, registering an appreciation that made her mouth feel suddenly dry. 'So that's what they mean by the "little black dress",' he remarked on an inflection of sardonic humour. 'Were you planning to start a riot?'

Shelley felt her cheeks colour a hot pink as she slid her hands self-consciously down over the smooth black fabric that skimmed her slender figure—and stopped quite a few inches above her knees. 'Is it too short?' she queried with an anxious frown. She hadn't worn this dress for a couple of years, and she had forgotten just how much leg it left on show.

'Not at all,' he responded in a tone that still left her in some doubt. 'It looks exactly the right length to me.'

Her green eyes flashed him a sharp warning. She was going to have to be very careful not to give him the wrong impression this evening, she reminded herself firmly—she had agreed to go out with him, but it was *not* a date.

'I'll. . .just pop and say goodbye to Emmy,' she managed a little shakily.

The child's room was just a step across the hallway from her own. She was already tucked up in her cot, with Auntie Winnie reading her bedtime story—subject to stern corrections every time she wavered by the slightest nuance from the standard text. She peeped up with her wide, rosy-cheeked smile as Shelley popped her head round the door.

'We'll be going now,' she said. 'Night-night, chick—be good.' The child yawned sleepily as she bent over the cot to drop a kiss on the golden curls. 'She shouldn't be any problem,' she added quietly to Winnie. 'She's had a long day—with a bit of luck she'll drop straight off.'

The elderly lady beamed with pleasure. 'Ah, don't you worry—I'll keep an eye on her,' she assured her comfortably. 'Off you go and have a nice time, the two of you.'

'Thank you,' Shelley murmured with a touch of wry humour. It hadn't taken her long to discover that Winnie doted on her employer—she had known him since he'd been Emma's age—and she had taken a sentimental delight in seeing him playing happy families; it was unfortunate that she was doomed to be disappointed.

'And don't you worry about hurrying home,' Winnie added in a tone that was almost conspiratorial. 'I shall be quite happy watching the late film.'

Shelley tucked the duvet up around Emma's shoulders, and bent to give her another kiss. But Emma had other ideas. 'Nuncle Saul!' she demanded imperiously.

He came forward, a look of puzzled enquiry on his face. Shelley smiled in wry apology. 'I think she wants a goodnight kiss,' she explained a little awkwardly.

'Oh. . .' By the soft glow of the night-light beside the cot it was difficult to read the expression in his eyes, but in tolerant response to the toddler's plea he leaned over the cot and dropped a kiss onto the tip of her little button nose. 'Goodnight, then, chicken,' he murmured. 'Sleep tight.'

Emma, content now, snuggled down beneath the duvet with another sleepy yawn, ready to hear the end of her story.

'We won't be late,' Saul assured Winnie, taking Shelley's arm in a casually possessive grip that she feared would only fuel the poor housekeeper's romantic hopes. 'Goodnight.'

Shelley let him lead her from the room, acutely conscious of his touch on her arm—it seemed to generate a strange tingle that ran through her like static electricity. As they walked down the stairs, she cast a covert glance up at him from beneath her lashes, admiring again the well-cut elegance of his formal dinner jacket, wondering for about the fiftieth time why he had invited her to go with him tonight—it certainly couldn't have been because he was short of a partner. . .

Dammit, she didn't *like* being so suspicious—it was against her nature. But, thanks to Colin, she had been forced to conclude that trusting was for fools.

But she could certainly get used to this kind of lifestyle, she mused as they reached the car. He opened the car door for her, and she sank into the comfort of the cream Connolly leather seat with a luxurious sigh. Everything about this car, from its smooth, sensual lines to the gleaming burr-walnut of the dashboard, breathed discreet luxury.

It was only the brightly coloured child-seat in the back that struck a note of incongruity, she mused with a touch of dry humour—a reminder of just how much a small child could disrupt the most well-ordered, sophisticated lifestyle. If Saul Rainer *was* harbouring any secret intentions of luring her into some kind of affair, he was going to have to understand that her daughter was part of the package—and if he didn't like it that was just too bad.

'Are you warm enough?' he enquired solicitously as he sparked the ignition and the wide tyres crunched softly over the gravel of the drive.

'Yes, thank you.' She sighed, leaning back and closing her eyes, trying to relax. This was just a moment in time, she tried to tell herself—something apart from the real world, something she ought to be able to allow herself to enjoy for its own sake. It was just her awkward conscience that wouldn't let her deny that even the most simple interchange with this man was imbued with a whole subtext of forbidden meanings.

She wasn't sure how far they were going, but the low purr of the engine spoke of an easy power that could eat up the miles at a speed that would hardly be noticed. Saul had put a CD in the player, and the cool jazz voice of Billie Holiday coiled around them like blue smoke as she closed her eyes and tried not to let herself be too conscious of the man beside her at the wheel.

It was about half an hour later that they turned off the main road and drove on for a short distance down a narrower lane until they came to a compound surrounded by a high chain-link fence, with a pair of wide gates that stood open. There were several cars ahead of them, and Shelley noticed that they had to stop to show some kind of pass before they were allowed in, but when it came to them they were waved through straight away with an informal salute.

Ahead of them was a building that looked rather like an aircraft hangar, smartly painted blue, with a large roller-shutter door at one end. Two giant pantechnicons in the racing team's livery of blue and white were parked beside it, and Saul slid the Aston Martin into a reserved space next to them, ignoring the car park, which was almost full.

She slanted a sardonic glance around at the scene. 'You sponsor all this?'

'I'm one of the main sponsors, but there are several other people involved.'

'Even so, it must cost a fortune.'

He shrugged in a gesture of casual dismissal. 'It's a hobby.'

'Some hobby,' she remarked drily.

He chuckled with laughter. 'You're a very difficult woman to impress.'

Her mouth tightened. Was that what he was trying to

do—impress her with his wealth and importance? Well, he was barking up the wrong tree—those weren't the kinds of things that impressed her. If he thought that was the way to get her into his bed, he was in for a severe disillusionment.

He had climbed out of the car, and was walking round to open the passenger door for her, but she preferred to scramble out by herself, ignoring the smile of mocking amusement that told her he was fully aware that she didn't want to have to give him her hand.

She really shouldn't have agreed to come, but it was too late to change her mind now. All she could do was try to get through the evening with as much dignity as she could manage—and try not to mind that everyone was going to assume that she was his latest bimbo. After all, she would never see any of them again, so it didn't really matter what they thought of her. Consciously drawing herself up to her full height, she swung her handbag across her shoulder, leaving him to follow her across the stone-paved patio outside the main entrance.

Another security guard was on duty just inside the door, checking passes before allowing people to enter, and Shelley hesitated a little awkwardly as he held out his hand for hers. But then Saul stepped forward, that possessive hand against her arm again, and instantly the guard waved them through.

'Don't forget you're with me,' he murmured, close to her ear. 'There are *some* advantages to it, you know.'

She wasn't quite sure how to respond to that, so she said nothing.

They had moved into a carpeted reception area, the walls of which were a display board for a fascinating photographic history of motor racing—black and white prints of men in leather helmets and bomber jackets posing beside long-bodied coupés on wind-swept airstrips, vivid colour shots of Lotuses and Ferraris at Le Mans and Monza, and autographed pictures of all the greats— Fangio, Sterling Moss, Nikki Lauda. . .

'Saul—darling! Where have you been hiding, you naughty man? Why weren't you at the track-testing this afternoon?'

Shelley turned sharply from the photographs to find herself displaced at Saul's side by a sizzling blonde in a sprayed-on pink catsuit, who wound herself around him like a Russian vine that was determined to cling on through the fiercest hurricane. And he didn't seem too upset about it, she noted tartly. Damn! There was that stupid jealousy again—and of a woman pumped up with so much silicone she probably couldn't lie face down in bed!

Well, she certainly wasn't going to give him the satisfaction of competing for his attention. But as she started to move away he shot out one arm, catching her around the waist and pinning her to his side. 'I'm sorry, Delia,' he responded to the blonde's challenge, smiling with that lazy charm that seemed to have every woman he met purring like a stroked kitten. 'I'm afraid I've been. . .otherwise engaged.'

Eyes like sharpened steel sliced a laser glare in Shelley's direction, but the voice was as sweet as honey as she pouted up at Saul. 'Ah, well, you're here now. Come on through and get some champagne. It's a fabulous party—there are *dozens* of photographers here.'

'Unfortunately most of them will be trying to get pictures of the car,' he teased her lightly. 'Oh, by the way, Shelley, this is Delia Sanderson—her husband is one of the other sponsors. Delia—Shelley.'

Shelley found herself subjected to a critical survey that

picked out every hand-set stitch of her home-made dress, before the other woman conceded a satisfied little smile. 'Shelley?' she repeated in a voice of smug condescension. 'Is that short for Michelle?'

Before she could reply, Saul laughed, that casually possessive arm drawing her closer against him. 'No, it's short for Percy,' he answered for her, his dark eyes smiling down into hers—and his hand on her waist seemed to be scorching her skin through the soft black satin of her dress. She shot him a look of angry resentment; he seemed determined to give the impression that there was a great deal more to their relationship than there was in reality, though he hardly needed to parade her as his latest conquest to enhance his deadly reputation.

Delia was frowning at him in puzzled confusion. 'Percy?' she repeated blankly. 'What do you mean?'

'Percy Bysshe Shelley,' Saul supplied with enigmatic amusement. 'You know—the nineteenth century poet,' he elucidated helpfully. 'Surely you remember? Ozymandias and all that.'

'Ozymandias? Oh. . .yes. . .of course. . .' Her blank expression indicated that she hadn't a clue what he was talking about, but she quickly recovered her glossy-lipped smile. 'Anyway, do come and join us,' she insisted, tugging on his arm. 'Ted's been droning on about all sorts of technical stuff, but now that you're here it'll be so much more fun.'

They walked through another set of doors, into a vast, barn-like space which Shelley guessed must be the main garage area. The floor was of concrete, and the walls and roof of ribbed metal, so that the background of rock music and the noise of a hundred people chattering echoed like a shifting thunderstorm over their heads.

The car that was at the centre of all the razzmatazz

was on a shoulder-high podium—a sleek blue and white
pod with wings and spoilers plastered with the logos of
all the sponsors, its wide, slick tyres still pitted from the
afternoon of track-testing it had had to undergo before
setting off for the first of the Formula Three races in a
few weeks' time. Shelley identified the drivers at once—
two arrogant-looking young men in blue and white racing
suits, draped with half a dozen skimpily dressed models,
as a posse of photographers used up roll after roll of film.

Saul forged a way through the crowd towards a group
standing close to the podium. Shelley felt her heart sink-
ing; this was everything she had feared. The men, like
Saul, were all wearing dinner jackets or business suits,
while the women reflected their status and bank accounts
with their expensive, salon-styled hair and elegant
designer clothes and their chic little Prada handbags.

Unfortunately, as she quickly realised, any hope she
might have had of fading into the background was
doomed from the start. It was partly her own fault—she
really shouldn't have worn such a short dress. But with
her height and her unruly cascade of russet hair she had
never been able to avoid notice anyway.

Saul made the introductions, and she tried hard to
remember the names and who was partnered by whom.
The conversation, naturally, was all about the cars. 'If
you're going to cut the downforce, of course that's going
to affect them on the corners.' The speaker was a heavily
set man in his middle forties—Delia's husband. 'There'll
be that much less drag, so even though the engines have
been down-specced they'll hit the same terminal
velocity. . . Oh, I'm sorry, my dear,' he added, turning
to Shelley with the kind of smug male condescension
that always irked her. 'I'm afraid all this technical stuff
must be terribly boring.'

'Not at all,' Shelley responded, returning the smile brightly. 'Won't less downforce make for better racing? Surely it'll give the driver a better feel of the road, and more warning if the car begins to break away?'

'Well, yes it will. . .' he conceded, startled to find that she had understood exactly what he was talking about. 'So, you're a fan of motor racing, then?'

'Not really—I prefer motor bikes. I used to ride one myself, in fact, until. . .fairly recently.' Until she'd been expecting Emma, but she chose not mention that. 'A Harley.'

'A Harley? Isn't that rather a big bike for a woman to manage?' he queried with a patronising smile.

She returned him a long, cool look. 'I managed it.'

The put-down had been irresistible, but she was a little afraid that she might have annoyed Saul by biting at his friend. She risked a swift glance up at him from beneath her lashes, to find him smiling at her—that heart-stopping smile that seemed to be just for her. Heaven help me, she prayed silently as she felt a blush of pink steal into her cheeks—I really am falling in love with him.

It seemed that the mention of motor bikes had touched a deep vein of interest—at least among the men. Shelley found herself the focus of all their attention—a fact which didn't go unnoticed by their wives and partners, whose glaring hostility openly accused her of deliberately playing it that way.

'I've always fancied one of those nice sporty little Italian jobs myself,' one of the others remarked. 'A Ducati—now there's a bike.'

'You can't beat a British bike,' the third insisted. 'Give me a Triumph any day. Best bike on the road. I like the Harley, though,' he added, as if afraid of offending

Shelley. 'I had a look at this new one they've brought out—the fuel-injection model. Great tourer.'

'I suppose it had to come,' Shelley said, with the purist's reluctant acceptance of progress. 'At least it meets the emissions spec without having to go for water-cooling. It ought to give it a bit more mid-range grunt as well. But I did like the old carburettor version, even if it sometimes needed a bit of persuasion at low revs,' she added wistfully.

Risking another glance up at Saul, she caught that smile again, the glint of appreciative amusement in those dark eyes, and had to look away again swiftly to prevent him from seeing the effect it had on her. Dear God, if he only had to *look* at her to make her bones melt. . .

'Champagne?' he offered, claiming two glasses from a passing waiter.

'Er. . .thank you,' she murmured, hoping a little desperately that he would assume the heated blush in her cheeks was caused by the warm crush of the crowd. She needed a drink to steady her nerves a little—not too much, though, she warned herself judiciously, recalling what had happened the first time she had met him. Tonight she had to be sure that she could stay in control. Not that she was afraid he would try to ply her with alcohol in order to take advantage of her, of course— that sort of underhand tactic wasn't his style. He would be far more subtle in his seduction.

Seduction. . . Even just thinking about the word made her mouth go dry. Standing beside him, forced close by the press of people around them, she was much too aware of his physical presence—his commanding height, the easily athletic way he moved, the hard-muscled breadth of his shoulders beneath the beautifully tailored dinner jacket. Even without closing her eyes, she could imagine what his body would be like—lean and hard, the skin sheened with bronze and scattered with rough, dark, curling male hair. . .

'Mr Rainer, could we have a few pictures?'

Shelley blinked, startled, as a flash-gun dazzled her from just a few feet away. Saul was smiling down at her, a glint of mocking amusement in his dark eyes, that possessive arm imprisoning her against his side. She barely had a chance to register what was happening before the photographer had reeled off another half-dozen shots, while the reporter who was with him had whipped out his notebook.

'Do you have any special plans for the new season, Mr Rainer?'

'We're looking forward to a lot of success,' Saul responded smoothly. 'We've got a good car and a good team, and two very competitive drivers—Hugh, of course, brings us experience, but Jean-Luc is very much looking to make his mark and move on to bigger things in due course.'

'Formula One?'

'I think he has the skill.'

'And any plans of your own, Mr Rainer?' he added cheekily, slanting a meaningful glance towards Shelley.

Saul laughed with the tolerant amusement of one for whom press intrusion came with the territory. 'If I have, you'll be the first to know.'

'Could I have the lady's name?' The pencil was poised expectantly, but Saul shook his head.

'You can just call her "a good friend".'

The reporter grinned knowingly. 'OK—thanks, Mr Rainer,' he responded, slithering away to seek out other prey.

Furious, Shelley pulled herself out of Saul's grasp. 'Why did you do that?' she demanded heatedly.

'What, let him take a few pictures?' he queried with a show of innocent surprise. 'He's only doing his job.'

'But why did you tell him to call me a good friend?' she choked out.

That hard mouth curved into a taunting smile. 'Would you rather I'd told him your name?'

'No!' she protested sharply. 'I'd rather you hadn't told him anything! I don't want my picture in the papers.'

He shrugged in casual unconcern. 'I'm afraid there's nothing I can do about it. Experience has taught me that the more you try to stop them publishing, the more they pursue you. It's best just to take no notice.'

'That's easy for you to say—you're used to it. But I'm not, and I...don't like it.' Drawing in an enraged breath, she glanced around, seeking for some excuse to escape. 'I... Excuse me, I need to go and comb my hair.'

This time he made no move to detain her. Threading her way through the crowd, she managed to find the ladies' room, and dived into one of the cubicles and bolted the door, leaning back against it and closing her eyes in relief. Just a few minutes' respite was all she needed—a chance to cool her face and steady the agitated beating of her heart.

Why was he behaving like this, as if they were already having an affair? Maybe because he knew just how seriously she was tempted. But she *couldn't* let herself give in to it; she knew all the reasons why not—she didn't need to remind herself of them. Unfortunately, knowing them made it no easier to keep the aching longings of her own heart under control. She was in serious danger of falling in love with him.

It was some time before she felt that she had recovered

sufficient composure to be able to go back outside again, but then, just as she was about to open the cubicle door she heard someone else come into the ladies' room, and immediately recognised Delia's voice, edged with spite.

'Saul's latest? I wouldn't have thought she was exactly his type, would you? I mean, those dreadful cheap earrings, for a start! And all that rubbish about motor bikes, just to get all the men eating out of her hand.'

Shelley hesitated, her heart thudding so loud that she was sure that the vicious blonde and whoever she was with would be able to hear it. She should just open the door, but what she had heard already would cause embarrassment enough. Besides, she wanted to hear what else they might have to say. . .

'Oh, I don't know,' the second woman responded lightly. 'She's certainly striking. Your Ted seemed to think so, anyway.'

'Oh, you know what men are.' Delia gave a harsh laugh. 'Anything in a skirt that short'll have them drooling like a St Bernard. It was positively indecent. And don't think your Pete didn't notice—he could barely take his eyes off her.'

The other woman was only amused by that attack, chuckling complacently. 'Pete always was a leg man. Though I'm not sure about her being Saul's latest—Pete told me she's married, with a little girl.'

'*Married?*' Delia sounded as if she had been punched in the stomach. 'But. . .he's always told me it was against his principles to have anything to do with a married woman!'

'Oh, I don't think you should feel as if your nose has been put out of joint,' the second woman assured her with spurious kindness. 'After all, Ted's one of his best friends—that does make rather a difference.'

'There's never been any question of Saul and I having an affair,' Delia protested, struggling for some kind of dignity. 'I wouldn't dream of being unfaithful to Ted.'

'Of course not. Anyway, Pete told me that her husband's turned out to be some kind of crook. He's stolen all her money—left her with nothing, Pete said. That's why she's staying at Saul's house.'

'Really?' Delia prompted her with interest as Shelley, hidden, wished the floor would open up and swallow her.

'Apparently this guy used to work for Saul, but he's embezzled a load of money from him as well, and disappeared.'

'Ah!' Delia laughed, hard and cynical. 'Well, that explains it, doesn't it?'

'What do you mean?' The second woman had asked the question that had sprung to Shelley's own lips.

'Well, some guy's run off with a pile of Saul's cash, and the next minute he's got the wife and kid tucked away down here all nice and cosy. You can bet your life *that's* not out of the goodness of his heart—not if I know Saul!'

'Well. . .no, I suppose not,' the other woman conceded. 'So what do you think is going on?'

'He's taking payment in kind, of course,' Delia surmised crudely. 'Saul never was the man to let anyone get one over on him—even if he's got so much money he's hardly going to notice the odd few hundred thousand going astray. But getting the wife to do jiggy-jig—now *that'd* be a brilliant way of getting revenge. . .' The voices faded as the two women went back outside.

Shelley felt suddenly sick. She leaned back against the door again, those last words still echoing in her ears— 'Getting the wife to do jiggy-jig. . .' They said eavesdroppers never heard anything good! But very often they heard the truth, she acknowledged bitterly—unvarnished by the niceties of social convention.

Was Delia right? Was Saul callously planning to use her for some kind of twisted revenge against Colin? She found it hard to believe. . .and yet. . . She had been afraid that she was too easily letting that smooth charm lure her into trusting him. Hadn't she learned her lesson? She had trusted Colin, and he had betrayed her—she ought to have taken that as a warning that she was a lousy judge of character.

She shook her head, struggling to calm the turmoil of emotions raging inside her. It really didn't make any difference anyway, she reminded herself sternly—she had already vowed not to surrender to that frighteningly powerful temptation he presented. She would just have to make very sure that she stuck to that resolve. Somehow.

CHAPTER SIX

IF SHELLEY was a little quiet on the way home, Saul seemed not to notice. It was fortunate that it was not too far. Cocooned with him in the luxurious comfort of the car, with the moonlight dusting the road ahead, she was finding it almost impossible to control her physical awareness of him. It was like something gnawing inside her. Watching his hands on the wheel, effortlessly controlling the powerful car, she could imagine them on her body, touching her, caressing her. . . She had to turn the low groan on her lips quickly into a yawn.

He glanced down at her, his dark eyes unreadable. 'Tired?'

'A little.'

'Well, we're home now.'

The wide wheels crunched over the gravel of the drive as he parked beside the front porch; then he climbed out to walk around and open her door for her. She hadn't intended to let him take her hand, but the seat was so low. . . As she rose to her feet, she tried to draw it away from him, but he wasn't about to let her go.

'Did you enjoy this evening?' he asked, his voice as soft as the moonlight.

He was so close that it was difficult to breathe, impossible to lift her eyes to meet his. 'Yes. . .thank you. . .'

'Did you?' His fingers laced into hers, and he lifted their entwined hands to look at them, as if their entanglement had nothing to do with him.

'Yes. . . I. . .' Her mouth was dry, and she knew he

111

must be able to feel the way she was trembling. She lifted her eyes to his in silent pleading for her freedom, but found herself instead more deeply snared in the web of magic he was spinning around her, trapped by that dark, mesmerising gaze.

'Did you. . .?' It was no more than a husky murmur as he feathered a kiss across each knuckle, and then drew her inexorably towards him, holding her close with no more than the power of his will. But as his mouth came down to claim hers she knew that she didn't want to escape.

It was a kiss of the deepest tenderness, and the sweetest temptation. His lips moved over hers in lingering enticement, coaxing them apart to allow his plundering tongue to swirl languorously over the delicate membranes within, stirring a wanton response inside her that she didn't know how to control. His arms wrapped around her, curving her slender body against his hard length, and the evocative musky scent of his skin was inveigling her senses with every ragged breath.

Vivid images were stirring in her mind—images of his powerful body entwined with hers, naked, crushing her beneath him, those hard muscles moving smoothly beneath his sun-bronzed skin as he held her, possessed her. . .

A low moan escaped her lips as her head tipped back, exposing the long, sensitive column of her throat to the scalding heat of his kisses, and she felt his hand move with unmistakable intent towards the firm, ripe curve of her breast, his long fingers brushing the aching swell with the lightest touch. The need inside her was like a physical pain, fierce and urgent. . .

But she couldn't let it happen, she reminded herself fiercely. She was a married woman—her conscience wasn't going to let her forget that. And besides, there were still so many doubts and questions. She didn't want to believe that Delia had been right, but how could she be sure? She could no longer trust her own fallible instincts.

Even so, it took every ounce of will-power she possessed to draw back from him, and, sensing the conflict inside her, he refused to release her from his arms.

'I want you,' he growled, his voice low and sensuously persuasive. 'I want to make love to you.'

'No. . .I. . . Please, Saul, let me go,' she begged brokenly, unable to lift her eyes to his, unable to free herself from his hold on her.

'You know you want to.'

'Yes.' How could she deny it? 'But. . .'

'But?' He lifted one dark eyebrow in sardonic question.

'I'm. . .not going to go to bed with you,' she forced out, struggling to sound convincing. 'I'm. . .married.'

He laughed in stinging mockery, his hands sliding down the length of her spine to curve her intimately against him as if to taunt her with a reminder of what she was refusing. 'Dammit, I know you're married,' he grated. 'But you're not in love with him—you were never in love with him.' It was a statement, not a question. 'You couldn't have kissed me like that if you were.'

Shelley hesitated, still reluctant to acknowledge a truth she knew was unavoidable. 'That's not the point,' she responded evasively. 'He's. . .my husband.' She finally managed to lift her eyes to meet his. 'I can't just pretend that he doesn't exist.'

He drew in a long, deep breath, as if struggling to maintain his own self-control. 'All right,' he conceded, finally letting her go. 'If that's the way it has to be. It

seems a little. . .ironic that you should have such high
principles, when he appears to have none at all.'

She stared at him, surprised and perversely a little
disappointed to have won the argument so easily—some
treacherous part of her had almost wanted him to ignore
her protests, to scoop her up in his strong arms and carry
her into the house and up the stairs to his bedroom, to
throw her onto the bed and make love to her so fiercely
that she would be absolved of any blame for not resisting.

'You're not. . .coming in yet?' she enquired a little
shakily as he turned away and started to walk off down
the path.

He shook his head. 'I'm going to take a walk—a long
one. Goodnight, Shelley.'

'G. . .goodnight.'

She had her own key, and she let herself into the house
as quietly as she could. Part of her—a weak, foolish
part—was aching to run back to him, to throw herself
into his arms and beg him to make love to her.

But she couldn't do that; there were far too many
barriers between them—not the least, a golden-haired
toddler sleeping peacefully in the room upstairs at the
end of the passage. She had lost a father and now, almost
certainly, a stepfather. She needed no more disturbance
in her young life at the moment.

The pleasant spring weather of the Easter weekend had
given way to April showers. Emma was in the kitchen,
'helping' Winnie make pastry, and Shelley had been on
her way upstairs to sort out the clothes that needed to
go into the laundry—but instead she had lingered at
the window on the first landing, gazing out over the
bedraggled garden and the choppy grey sea. She had
been here for over half an hour now, thinking about

nothing in particular—that seemed to be happening quite a lot these past few days.

Suddenly the low growl of a car's engine caught her attention, and her heart thumped. There was no mistaking the sound of Saul's car.

It was almost a week since she had seen him—well, four days, eleven hours and twenty-five minutes, actually. He had left on the Sunday morning before even Emma had been awake—she had heard his quiet footsteps on the stairs, heard the front door open and close, heard the car drive away, and she had lain in bed trying to tell herself that she had done the right thing, the sensible thing. So why did doing the right thing have to hurt so much?

What was he doing here, in the middle of a working day? He hadn't said he would be coming back this week. . . Resolutely she pushed aside the forbidden thoughts that crept unbidden into her mind, and, drawing in a long, deep breath in an effort to steady the ragged beating of her heart, she went down to the hall to meet him as he came through the door.

'Hello.' Was her smile a little too bright? 'I wasn't expecting you. . .'

He returned the smile, though his eyes remained dark. 'I've had some more news,' he responded.

'About Colin?'

He nodded grimly. 'Remember I told you they'd traced your money? Well, he's started to draw on it—a cheque was cashed yesterday. In Edinburgh.'

'Edinburgh?' she repeated, frowning. 'What on earth would he be doing up there?'

'I don't know—but I intend to find out.' His voice was as hard as steel. 'Of course, there's no guarantee he's still there, but it's as good a starting point as any.'

'You're going up there yourself?' she queried, startled.

'We don't have any pictures of him,' he reminded her drily. 'My agents are good, but with only a description to go on it'll be damned nearly impossible for them to find him. At least I know what he looks like.'

'I'm coming with you.' The martial glint in her eyes warned him not to argue. 'I know what he looks like too—a lot better than you do. And I'm certainly not going to sit here tamely while everyone else gets all the excitement.'

He laughed, shaking his head. 'I didn't think you would. But what about Emma? I don't think it would be a terribly good idea to take her with us.'

Shelley hesitated, frowning; he had a point—it wouldn't be fair on the child to drag her around with them while they looked for Colin. There was Winnie, of course—but though the elderly housekeeper doted on the child a few hours of her lively presence was more than enough to exhaust her.

'She can go and stay with Dad and Eileen for a few days,' she decided.

Saul lifted one dark eyebrow in quizzical enquiry. 'I thought you didn't get on with your stepmother?'

'I don't,' Shelley acknowledged with a quirk of wry humour. 'But she dotes on Emma—she'll be more than happy to have her. She'll probably spoil her rotten!'

'OK. How long will it take you to get ready?'

'Not long—I just have to pack a few things for me and Emma. She's playing in the kitchen with Winnie at the moment.'

'OK. There's no rush,' he assured her. 'We might as well have a bite to eat before we go. It's a long drive. Shall we say one o'clock?'

'That'll be fine.' But though there was no reason to

hurry she ran up the stairs, taking them two at a time, her mind ticking off the items she would need to pack. She wasn't going to let herself pause for long enough to think about the reasons why she shouldn't be going to Edinburgh with Saul, in case her common sense stopped her doing it.

It had been the middle of the night when they had arrived in Scotland's capital, and Shelley had been too tired to be sure that the floodlit castle she had glimpsed high on its rocky crag right in the very centre of town—or even the hotel itself with its marbled hall and grand stairway, and its air of hushed luxury—had been anything more than a dream.

But, waking in a wide bed to find herself surrounded by Edwardian elegance, and padding barefoot across the deep-pile carpet to draw aside the heavy swags of the curtain to peep out of the window, she knew that it was all real—though she could see why she would have been confused.

Even in the pale sunlight, the castle looked like something out of a Ruritanian fantasy; its hard grey walls and crenellated rooves seemed to grow straight out of the sheer granite face of the peak on which it stood. Far below it, falling away to the left, was a wide green slash of parkland and trees, which rose again to railings and flag-poles and a bustling street of smart shops, as fashionable as any of those in London's West End. The contrast between ancient and modern was so startling that she had to look back again to try to grasp it—it was as if a thousand-year gap of history faced itself across the tops of the trees.

A soft tap on the door brought her head around, and she quickly snatched up the white towelling dressing gown, bearing the hotel's discreet blue logo, that she had discarded at the foot of the bed when she had crawled exhausted between the sheets after the long drive.

'Wait a minute,' she called, wrapping the tie belt around her waist and swiftly rifling her fingers through her tangled hair. And then, drawing in a long, deep breath, she pulled open the door.

Saul stood in the doorway, regarding her with a smile of lazy mockery that had a damaging effect on her composure—such as it was. 'Good morning, sleepyhead,' he remarked. 'You finally decided to wake up, then?'

She blinked the last of the sleep from her eyes, stepping back automatically as he came into the room. 'What time is it?'

'A quarter to ten. I thought you were going to sleep all day.'

She shook her head, a little surprised to learn that it was so late. 'I don't usually get a lie in—Emma has me awake by six most days. I suppose I've missed breakfast?'

'Call Room Service,' he advised with casual unconcern. 'They'll bring you anything you fancy.'

Shelley frowned, glancing again around the spacious room, twice the size of her sitting room at home, and furnished with tasteful—and very expensive—elegance. 'How much is this room costing?' she enquired bluntly.

He brushed the question aside with a dismissive shrug of his wide shoulders. 'It doesn't matter.'

'It does,' she insisted with brittle dignity. 'When I said I wanted to come up here with you, I didn't mean for you to fork out for my expenses. I can find somewhere cheaper to stay.'

'That wouldn't be convenient. We need to concentrate

on finding Colin, not dashing around looking for cheap digs for you.'

She glared back at him, as obstinate as he. 'Then tell me how much it costs, and I'll pay you back.'

'How?' he returned, an inflection of sardonic humour in his voice.

'When I get my money back from Colin,' she asserted grittily. 'I don't like. . .being beholden to anyone.'

'Whatever you say,' he conceded, his eyes glinting with something like amusement. He had strolled across the room to drop himself into one of the two wing-chairs that flanked the tall window. 'So if you'd care to get dressed we can start looking.'

She returned him a look of sharp suspicion—she had expected far more of an argument. Well, he needn't think he was going to avoid letting her pay him back when the time came—though she was uncomfortably aware that it was going to eat a rather large hole in whatever money she managed to recover from Colin. But that problem could wait.

'Do you really think he's still here?' she asked, glancing around and remembering that she had hung her clothes in the mirrored closet in the lobby between the bedroom and the bathroom.

'Possibly not. But it's a big town—he may have been hoping to be able to lie low for a while.'

'How do you plan to find him?'

'I have a feeling that he may find us,' his voice responded lazily.

'What do you mean?' she queried as she chose a long black sweater and a short black skirt from the closet, and opened a drawer to pick out some underwear.

'He's bound to guess that I'll come looking for him sooner or later, so if he *is* here he's likely to be keeping

an eye on this hotel—he'd know this would be where
I'd stay. But he won't have been expecting you to be
with me, and when he finds out that we're sharing a
suite. . .'

Shelley stepped back through the door, clutching her
bundle of clothes, her eyes wide and startled. 'What do
you mean, sharing a suite?' she demanded sharply.

He smiled slowly, his dark eyes mocking. 'Two bed-
rooms, two bathrooms, one sitting room,' he enumerated,
counting on his fingers. 'Of course, you have your own
door onto the corridor, as well as the one into the private
lobby between your room and mine. And your room has
its own lock. But it's a suite.' He leaned back in the
armchair, his arms folded and his long legs stretched out
across the carpet, as comfortably at home as he was
entitled to be, since he was paying for the room. 'I
thought you were getting dressed?'

'I don't want to share a suite with you!' she protested
vigorously.

'You don't have to worry,' he assured her with cool
amusement. 'I told you, your door has its own lock—if
you feel the need to use it. I shan't intrude. Unless, of
course, I'm invited. . .'

She felt her cheeks flame a heated red, and retreated
swiftly to the bathroom—which also had a lock, which
she used. Had he planned it this way? Had he come down
to Chichester to tell her what was going on, instead of
simply phoning, knowing that she would insist on coming
to Edinburgh with him?

Dammit—how could she be in love with a man she
didn't trust? Or did the fact that she *was* in love with
him mean that she really could trust him? Or maybe. . .
Or maybe she'd go completely mad if she kept going
round in circles, trying to reach a logical answer to some-

thing that defied logic, she scolded herself crisply. The best thing to do was simply go with the flow, and wait and see what happened.

With that resolution firmly in mind, she turned on the shower and stepped under the warm needles, soaping herself all over with a fragrant blue shower gel that she had found in a basket of freebies on the vanity shelf. After all, she argued to herself, since she was here she might as well make the most of the little luxuries provided.

The city looked as stunning from the castle as the castle did from the city. High on the windswept battlements, Shelley could look down on the narrow medieval jumble of the Royal Mile, or across the gracious width of Princes Street to the elegantly laid-out squares of the Georgian New Town—and then far beyond to where the grey waters of the Firth of Forth flowed out to the open sea.

It had been Saul's suggestion that they amuse themselves by going out to see the sights, and though it had seemed to her not to be what they were here for she had suspected that it would be a waste of breath to argue with him. It had certainly been worth the climb up the steep paths cut into the granite cliff from the gardens below—a climb she had been determined to make without having to resort to accepting his offer of a hand to help her up the toughest bits.

The only problem was that she had an uncomfortable feeling that she was being watched. It had begun not long after they had left the hotel and crossed the road to walk down into Princes Street Gardens. Maybe it was just the eerie old cemetery they had passed, with its silent watch-tower standing vigil over the ancient graves. . .

Impatiently she thrust such foolish thoughts out of her

mind—she had quite enough to worry about, without thinking about ghosts. 'What's that?' she asked, pointing to a strange black and white tower crowned with a dome, which stood at the far end of the Castle Esplanade, at the top of the Royal Mile.

'It's the Camera Obscura,' Saul told her. 'It's fascinating—do you want to go and have a look?'

'I suppose we might as well,' she conceded, shrugging her slim shoulders. So much for looking for Colin, she mused wryly—the morning was already slipping away, and so far they had made no effort whatsoever.

Any objections were quickly forgotten, however, as they climbed up the steep stairs inside the tower of the Camera Obscura. The sepia-tinted prints of the city's history were fascinating enough, but even more so was the hall of holographs, magical pictures of luminous green that sprang into dramatic three-dimensional life as she moved slowly past them.

'Oh, I must bring Emma here when she's older!' she declared, gazing in astonishment at a lifelike owl on outstretched wings that seemed to be flying right out of its frame. 'She'd love this.'

'This isn't the best bit,' Saul told her. 'Come on—it's nearly time for the show. You can look at the rest of these on the way down.'

Puzzled, she followed him up the rest of the stairs. It was early in the season, so there were not too many tourists—she could imagine that it would be packed later in the year. About a dozen of them shuffled into a small, round, darkened room and sat on benches around a plain white dish about a metre and a half across.

And then the operator closed the door, turning off the last light as she greeted them cheerily, and suddenly, there around the edge of the dish, was a moving panorama of the scene outside in shadowy colours, the sky in the middle a hazy blue. 'I'm sorry—it isn't very sunny today so the picture isn't so bright,' she explained, swinging a black metal rod that hung down from the centre of the high dome above the dish, so that the images moved. 'Look, there's the castle—they're just getting ready to change the guard.'

And there they were, the tiny figures of the soldiers that Shelley had seen just a few moments ago in their sentry-boxes at the castle gates, marching in ceremonial formation as the crowd of tourists paused to snap them with cameras, unaware that above and behind them unseen eyes were watching from the top of the black and white tower.

No wonder she had felt as if she was being watched, she mused with a quirk of wry self-mockery. She had been—but not by anything remotely sinister, merely an earlier audience here on these hard wooden benches! With a silent sigh of relief, she sat forward, amused by the games the operator was playing by sliding a piece of paper across the dish so that it looked as if she were scooping up people and cars as they went innocently about their business down below.

Suddenly she tensed. In the shadow of the corner where Castle Hill opened out into the wide Esplanade, on the far side from the Princes Street Gardens, one tiny figure had caught her eye. It had been just a fleeting glimpse—when she looked again, he was gone—but it had looked like Colin.

She glanced up at Saul, but he did not seem to have noticed—but then he didn't really know Colin particularly well. Maybe she had been mistaken—from this distance the shadowy figures were so small, and she had been looking down almost from above. Perhaps her mind had conjured the image of what she had been half expecting to see.

She hesitated about telling Saul of the incident. For one thing, she wasn't absolutely sure of what she had seen—if it really had been Colin, no doubt he would appear again sooner or later. In the meantime, she would just continue to go with the flow. . .

'Lunch?' Saul suggested as they left the Camera Obscura and began to stroll down Castle Hill. Shelley nodded. 'Restaurant or pub?'

'I don't mind,' she responded. 'You choose.'

'There's a nice pub along here—it's very popular with the tourists but at this time of year it shouldn't be too crowded. And they do a good meal.'

'Sounds fine to me.'

As they walked, she was trying to catch a glimpse in the shop windows opposite to see if anyone was following them. But if Colin was there he was being careful to stay out of sight. All the same, it made her feel uncomfortable—or was that just a guilty conscience?

The pub that they went to was in one of the narrow cobbled alleyways that led off each side of the Royal Mile, where the tall old houses clung to the side of the granite crag; in places the slope was so steep that the constricted passageways turned to steps. Ahead, between the stern grey walls of the tenements, Shelley could glimpse the rich green of Princes Street Gardens, and beyond that the shops of Princes Street itself.

And there, extending to a good fifty feet of frontage, was one of the Rainer superstores, with its distinctive electric-blue sign right along the top of the plate-glass window. It felt odd to be standing here looking at it with the man who owned it standing right beside her—a little as people must feel when meeting a celebrity whose face was as familiar as if they were a member of their family when in fact they were total strangers.

She glanced up at him, laughing lightly. 'Do you ever go into one of them and pretend to be just an ordinary customer, to see if they're on their toes?' she asked.

'Frequently.' His dark eyes glinted with amusement. 'But I give praise where it's due as well—several of my senior staff are in their present positions because they managed to impress me when I dropped in on them unannounced. I sometimes check out the opposition in the same way too—I wouldn't like to let them steal a march on me.'

He opened the door of the pub and she stepped inside. It was quite dark, the lights being shaded by heavy orange glass globes and the walls panelled with aged oak to the low, beamed ceiling. At the back was a massive fireplace, big enough to roast an ox, where a log fire sizzled and snapped, throwing out a heat so fierce that it would be difficult to sit close to it.

'What would you like to drink?' Saul enquired, steering her towards the bar with a casually possessive hand on her arm.

'Oh. . .a half of bitter, please,' she responded without thinking—and then almost bit her tongue as the glint of quizzical humour in his eyes reminded her that the type of girl he usually went out with would never dream of asking for beer. Well, so what? She didn't much like spirits, and she certainly wasn't going to change her tastes to suit him.

'A half of bitter it is,' he conceded, slanting her a teasing smile.

The menu was chalked on a board behind the bar; Shelley was pleased to see that it avoided the hackneyed tourist feature of haggis, but there were several other, less

well-known Scots classics—Partan Bree, Cabbie Craw,
Arbroath Smokies. She decided to settle for wild salmon,
which arrived in wafer-thin strips of soft pink flesh, with
squares of brown bread, on a bed of salad. With the cool,
strong beer it was delicious.

'Good?' Saul queried, smiling at the expression of
delight on her face as the fish almost melted in her mouth.

'Fantastic!' she approved readily. 'What's yours like?'

Saul had chosen Cabbie Craw, and he held out a bite
to her on his fork. She leaned across the table and took
it into her mouth. 'Mmm! What is it? Haddock?'

He nodded. 'Haddock dried in the open air—then they
boil it, and serve it with an egg sauce. It's one of my
favourite dishes.'

'And people think the only thing you get to eat in
Scotland is porridge!'

It was pleasantly companionable, sitting here in the
warmth from the fire, sharing the unpretentious meal.
But Shelley couldn't totally relax; she had made sure
when they'd sat down that she could see the door, and
as they ate she watched discreetly over Saul's shoulder.
There was no sign of Colin—but he could be somewhere
outside, waiting until they had finished their lunch. . .

Dammit, *they* were supposed to be following *him*, not
the other way round! But, as Saul had said, perhaps he
was wondering what she was doing here with him. Perhaps he was wondering if they were having an affair.

'I. . .suppose you must have been here quite often?'
she asked, trying to take her mind off the man she was
having difficulty thinking of as her husband. 'To
Edinburgh, I mean—and Scotland in general.'

He nodded. 'We've got shops in nearly all the larger
towns—three here in Edinburgh, in fact, and two in
Glasgow. Then there's a factory here, just outside the

town, that produces a lot of our own-brand stuff, and another one up in Aberdeen that makes the cases for the video and audio tapes before they're shipped down to Peterborough where the tapes themselves are produced.'

'I thought it was just shops you owned?' she queried, surprised.

'Oh, the retail division's quite a small part of the company. We manufacture our own range of white goods— fridges, washing machines, that sort of thing—as well as the home entertainments side. There's a factory in Holland, and another one in Italy, and we've just set one up in the Czech Republic to produce computers. Then we manufacture under licence for a lot of the other big names in the electrical business as well.'

She opened her eyes wide in surprise. 'It's a lot bigger than I thought! And you've managed all that in ten years?'

'I had a good reason to succeed.' For a moment a shadow darkened his eyes, and when he spoke again his voice was hard. 'My grandfather started the business— he used to have a few small electrical repair shops. My father took it over from him, and started to expand. He was doing pretty well—until he came into competition with one of the bigger boys. He fought them off for as long as he could, but they squeezed him until he was practically bankrupt—in the end they forced him to sell out to them for a pittance. The following year he had a stroke, and died. He was fifty-one.'

Shelley opened her mouth to speak, but she wasn't sure quite what to say. She would have offered sympathy, but she sensed the bitter anger beneath the surface—an anger that was the fuel-source for his fierce ambition.

'I was still in my teens,' he went on grimly, 'but I promised myself then that I was going to get back control. I started with a van, renting out videos door-to-door, then I got some shops, and when satellite television came in I started doing dishes. Ten years ago, I got my chance. I'd waited a long time, but I'd been watching them, and I knew just when they were overstretching themselves. I got them like that. . .'

He laid his hand on the table, face up, and slowly clenched his fingers into a choking grip. 'Every one of the directors who had been there when they took over my father I sacked personally—leaving the managing director till last. He was an arrogant son-of-a. . . He tried to tell me I needed him more than he needed me. The last I heard,' he added, smiling as he raised his glass of beer to his lips, 'he was trying to sell double glazing.'

Shelley felt a small shiver run down her spine. She had sensed when she had first met him that this man was dangerous. And Colin had been stupid enough to try to take him on! Fool! Saul would take him apart with the same kind of cold, calculating efficiency that he had used to take apart his former business enemies. He was completely ruthless, and anyone who cheated or crossed him would pay the price.

And could a man like that ever fall in love? Could he ever be willing to take the risk of being gentle as well as strong, of trusting someone else, of accepting her fallibilities as well as her strengths—of being prepared to risk getting hurt? Maybe. . . But she would probably never know the answer, she reminded herself crisply. Maybe one day she'd read in the newspapers that their playboy darling had finally decided to settle down, and she'd smile a little wistfully, remembering a few precious days in Edinburgh. . .

*　　*　　*

After lunch they went for a stroll around the Old Town. They visited the Writer's Museum, in one of the cobbled courtyards hidden among the tangle of wynds and closes that honeycombed both sides of the main road, and then walked down the hill to see the statue that had been erected to Greyfriars Bobby, the little Skye Terrier whose devotion to his master's grave had become a legend of the city.

'I'd like to get that story for Emma,' Shelley mused as they walked back up the hill towards the hotel.

'Well, there must be a dozen bookshops along Princes Street,' Saul told her. 'Why don't you take a look? I'll be busy this afternoon—I have some calls to make to New York.'

She hesitated for a moment. If Colin was still following them—if he *had* been following them—he might try to approach her once she was on her own. But then. . .why should she fear that? Colin would never hurt her. And besides, though she could think of no possible explanation that could account for what he had done, she ought to at least give him a hearing—after all, she was married to him.

But she didn't share her thoughts with Saul—she somehow doubted that he would appreciate her reasoning. 'All right,' she agreed, avoiding his eyes a little uneasily—it was unnerving that he always seemed able to guess what she was thinking. 'I'll see you later, then.'

But though she spent a pleasant hour or so strolling along the wide thoroughfare, gazing into shop windows, admiring clothes she couldn't afford, she saw no sign of Colin at all. She chose a brightly illustrated story book for Emma, reflecting ruefully that until everything was sorted out she would have to be careful even about such small purchases, and then hopped onto one of the open-topped tourist buses which took her for a circuit around the town before going back to the hotel.

It was a little intimidating to walk up to the sumptuous entrance beneath the porticoed frontage—she was conscious that the wind on the upper deck of the bus had whipped her hair into a bedraggled mess. But the doorman in his St Andrew's blue livery and top hat greeted her as politely as if she had been a princess, the hint of a twinkle in his eye letting her know that he was quite used to guests who did not quite look the part.

Their suite was on the first floor, so she climbed the stairs instead of using the lift. Rather than use the door into the lobby she shared with Saul, she went to her own door, but as she pushed it open a small piece of paper slid with it. She bent to pick it up, intrigued. It was folded to show a printed advertisement for a guided night walk around the sites of the city's gruesome history, but when she unfolded it she found a handwritten note on the back. The writing was Colin's. She read:

My darling Shelley, This letter is so hard to write. I know I should have explained everything to you before, but I couldn't bear to upset or worry you and I thought I would be able to sort things out without having to resort to drastic measures. Please believe me that I had very good reasons for what I've done, and I will pay you back every penny I've borrowed as soon as all this business is over. I know you're with Saul Rainer, and I do hope he's being kind to you, but please be very careful about how much you trust him— I have reason to know that he can be a very dangerous man. If you can get away, come on this walk tonight and I will find you. Please, please, Shelley, trust me, and everything will be all right. I love you, and always will. Your husband, Colin.'

She read it and reread it, frowning. What was she supposed to make of it? It really said nothing beyond a set of platitudes. The only concrete thing in it was the request that she should meet him tonight on this tour of the Old Town. She turned the paper over, glancing again at the advertisement. Eight o'clock, from the Mercat Cross next to the cathedral. Should she go? And, more to the point, should she tell Saul?

A glance at her watch told her that it was almost half past five. She had a couple of hours yet to think about it, to make up her mind. . .

CHAPTER SEVEN

A COLD, damp mist swirled around the ancient cathedral of St Giles. Shelley shivered inside her coat. It was a small party that stood at the foot of the Mercat Cross—a Japanese couple, and an American couple with their teenage daughter—listening to their guide's blood-curdling tales of the savage executions that had taken place here in years long past.

Shelley would have preferred it to have been a much larger group—not only was it rather spooky being almost alone in the dark, enveloping mist, but she felt much too exposed. Was Colin here, lurking unseen in the shadows, watching her?

And what about Saul? She hadn't told him where she was going, or even that she was going out—she had been afraid that he would try to stop her, or maybe insist on coming with her, and she'd known that if she didn't come alone Colin wouldn't show up. Fortunately Saul had been busy taking a series of calls from New York, and she had simply told him that she would see him later—hopefully he would just assume that she was somewhere in the big hotel. If he found out that she had sneaked out, and why. . .

Uneasily she peered over her shoulder, searching the doorways and alleyways across the street, but there was no one there. . .just the occasional echoing sound of foot-steps, or a spill of laughter and music from one of the pubs or restaurants further down the hill. If Colin was here, why didn't he just come over and join her? He had had time by now to check that she was alone.

The group moved on into the shadow of the cathedral, to hear another story—this one about the ghost of a hanged man which, it was said, still tried to crawl up the stone steps to seek sanctuary within the cathedral's doors. Their guide was a pale-faced young woman with long dark hair, who swirled her black cloak around her shoulders and rolled the spine-chilling legends off her tongue in a soft Edinburgh brogue that lent them a vivid authenticity, as if she had actually been there to witness the scenes she described.

Leaving the cathedral and the wide and comparatively well-lit high street behind, they now plunged down into the maze of narrow wynds, shadowed by the tall houses that loomed on each side of them. The American woman gave a nervous laugh as unconsciously the group bunched closer together; footsteps seemed to follow them, but they could have been no more than an echo of their own. The damp was creeping inside Shelley's coat, and she hugged it closer around herself, wondering if Colin would appear, wishing she were safe and warm in the hotel.

Had Saul realised yet that she wasn't there? It would depend, probably, on whether he had finished his business with New York. It would be dinnertime—perhaps he would be sitting down in the lushly luxurious dining room, his every whim being anticipated by waiters in formal dinner jackets and bow-ties, being serenaded by the music of the grand piano that she had glimpsed in the corner when she had peeped in earlier in the afternoon.

He would probably be furious when he found out what she had done. Well, that was just unfortunate, she told herself defiantly—he might be able to dictate to most people, but she wasn't going to let him dictate to her.

Although she had an uncomfortable suspicion that it was a great deal easier to contemplate defying him when he wasn't around than when face to face with him.

She shivered again, only half listening to the sepulchral tones of the guide as she related the legend of the piper who had gone down into a secret tunnel beneath the castle, never to be seen again—but still on a dark, windy night the sound of his pipes could be heard beneath the paving stones that now covered the ancient graveyard around St Giles Cathedral. . .

'You mean he just disappeared?' the American woman queried in wavering tones. 'Didn't they send someone to look for him?'

'Oh, yes,' the guide confirmed, her voice softly sibilant as a ghost's. 'A whole troop of guards were sent into the tunnel after him, with torches. But when they got to the point beneath the cathedral graveyard, the tunnel ended—and of the lone piper, there was no sign! So they bricked the tunnel up, and to this day no one has ever ventured down it again.'

'I'm not surprised!' the American woman declared with a satisfied shudder. 'Catch me going down into a place like that!'

Shelley smiled to herself. It was all just a lot of nonsense, of course. It wasn't the stories that were making the skin at the nape of her neck prickle—it was the sensation that she was being watched. She was quite sure of it now—and it was much stronger than it had been this afternoon. But where was he. . .?

As the guide led the party off again through the dark, narrow passageways, she hung back a little, listening for footsteps. 'Colin?' she whispered tensely. But there was no reply, just the voice of the guide weaving yet another narrative, and the rattle of an old beer can rolling in the gutter.

They were coming towards the end of the tour. Was he waiting until the others were gone? That is, if it *was* Colin. . . Following a little behind the group, she spun around quickly, hoping to catch him, but all she saw was the crooked outline of a medieval house that jutted out across the pavement, and the orange glow of a streetlight haloed in the mist.

The last port of call was an old cemetery. The American woman had to be coaxed to step through the creaking wrought iron gates, but her reluctance was overborne by her eager desire to be terrified out of her wits. Shelley's ambivalence was more prosaic—she was beginning to get more than a little annoyed with Colin for playing games with her like this, scaring her by creeping along behind without being seen. He could quite easily have joined her at any point during the walk, once he had been sure that Saul wasn't with her—provided, of course, that he paid his fee to the canny Scots lass, who certainly wouldn't have let anyone tag along for free.

The cemetery was a most suitable place to end the tour. One weak light on the side of the old church cast a feeble glow over ancient tombstones covered with damp moss and creepers, and beyond the bare trees and spiky iron railings that surrounded it the imagination could easily conjure the spectral shapes of the notorious nineteenth-century grave-robbers and murderers, Burke and Hare, going about their nefarious nightly business.

What a place for a secret tryst with a fugitive husband, Shelley mused wryly as she followed the little group through the gates. It was getting quite late now, and there were few people around; in the distance she could see the lights of Princes Street, but it seemed like another world.

She hovered on the fringe of the group as the guide spun her last story, peering uneasily around. There were so many shadows. . . Was that a movement she caught out of the corner of her eye? No, just the branch of an ancient willow, creaking in the cold night air. But there was someone here, watching her—she could feel him. . .

Suddenly she realised that the guide's recital had come to an end, and everyone else was leaving—leaving her behind. She stepped forward quickly to catch them up, but the distinct sound of a twig cracking underfoot spun her back.

'Colin. . .?' she queried tremulously, peering into the swirling mist. She didn't believe in ghosts—of course she didn't. It just wasn't logical. . .but there was *something* there. And then from behind a praying angel with folded wings a solid shape detached itself. 'Colin, is that you?' But it wasn't Colin—it was much too tall, too wide in the shoulder. . .

'So you *were* expecting to meet him here?' demanded a husky, hard-edged voice.

'*Saul?*' Shelley had never fainted in her life, but she felt uncomfortably close to it now. 'Was it. . .was it you who's been following me?'

'I've been following you since you left the hotel,' he responded curtly. 'I was a little. . .curious to know why you should be sneaking out at this time of the evening.'

'I wasn't sneaking!' she protested, struggling to steady the racing beat of her heart. 'I. . .'

'Yes?' he queried, icily polite, awaiting her explanation.

'I don't have to justify myself to you,' she asserted, returning him a look of haughty defiance.

'No?' He came slowly towards her, his feet crunching slightly on the gravel of the cemetery path. 'Six hundred thousand pounds of my money says you do.' Those dark eyes were blazing with an anger that made her heart thud in alarm, but as she stepped back he reached out and grasped her shoulders in a fierce grip that she could feel bruising her soft skin even through the thickness of her coat and sweater.

'You're hurting me.'

'Hurt you? I could kill you,' he growled, shaking her so hard that she felt her teeth rattle. 'Answer my questions, damn you. Were you planning to meet your husband here? Have you been a part of this all along? The poor little wife, cheated and dumped, playing on my sympathy, turning me on with kisses like honey while holding me at arm's length with your bleating about loyalty and guilt, until I can't damned well think straight any more!'

And then, before she had time even for a gasp of protest, he dragged her roughly against him, and his mouth came down on hers, hard and insistent, crushing her lips apart.

The hot savagery of it took her so much by surprise that she didn't even struggle—she could only surrender to the fierce demand, all the aching longing inside her sweeping aside any constraints as she curved herself against him, her hands lifting as if of their own volition to fold around his neck, her fingers sliding into the crisp hair at the nape of his neck.

His tongue swirled into her mouth in a plundering invasion, sweeping into every deep, sweet corner, igniting her responses. Her body was on fire, her blood racing in her veins, and she could hear her own ragged breathing as she clung to him, the searing heat of his kiss branding her soul with his mark of possession.

His hand had tangled in her hair, dragging her head

back as his mouth traced a scalding path down the long, vulnerable column of her throat. She was dizzy, racked with fever, the unique, musky scent of his skin inveigling her senses, filling her mind with wild images—images of that lean, hard body, the muscles smooth beneath sun-bronzed skin, entwined with hers, naked. . . And as his hand slid down the length of her spine, crushing her hard against him, she was made devastatingly aware of the warning tension of male arousal in him. Dear God, was he going to lay her back across one of these cold, damp tombstones, make love to her right here in the cemetery? And if he did, would she even try to stop him?

But he too must have realised how crazy that would be, and she sensed the effort of will it cost him as he brought the hot urgency under control. At long last he lifted his head, dragging in a harsh breath as his eyes glittered down into hers. 'God, I can't believe how much you can make me want you,' he grated. 'You can't be acting this.'

'I. . .I'm not,' she whispered, her voice unsteady. 'I haven't lied to you—I'm not a part of whatever Colin's done.'

'So what were you doing coming out to meet him like this?' he demanded roughly.

She hesitated, and then put her hand into her pocket and pulled out the note, handing it to him without a word. He moved over to the pool of light shed by the single lamp fixed to the church wall, holding the paper up to read it, his frown deepening as he tried to make sense of it. 'What a load of drivel!' he exploded. 'Trust him? You might as well trust a rattlesnake! Surely you didn't believe a word of this?'

'No, I didn't,' she retorted, stung to anger by his high-handed manner. 'I just. . .I thought I ought to give him a chance to. . .explain.'

'Explain?' He threw up his hand in a gesture of exasperation. 'What could he possibly say to explain tricking you into signing away your house and damned nearly every penny you owned?'

'I don't know!' Suddenly she was close to tears; why were they shouting at each other, when just a moment ago they had been kissing like the last lovers left on earth? 'Anyway, how did you know I'd left the hotel?' she demanded abruptly.

He conceded a wry smile. 'The. . .er. . .private inquiry agent who's been watching you all afternoon was waiting in Reception—she reported back to me as soon as she saw you leave.'

'The *what*? You didn't tell me about that!' she protested, furious.

'I told you I was employing a firm of private investigators to track Colin,' he reminded her coolly.

'Yes, but. . .you never told me they were going to be here, following me, spying on me!'

'Not spying on you,' he assured her in patient tones. 'Just watching to see if Colin would try to approach you.'

'You're just using me as bait,' she accused him bitterly. Suddenly a whole lot of questions were finding answers—answers that were not particularly welcome. 'That's why you took me to that party and let them take those photographs for the papers, isn't it—so Colin would see them? In fact, that's probably why you invited me down to stay in your house in the first place. I suppose you had one of your *private investigators* watching me the whole time?'

'Teams of two—in round-the-clock shifts,' he

admitted with blunt honesty. 'They've been following us both all the time we've been up here.'

'Damn you!' she cried, furious with herself for letting herself be fooled by him. 'I knew there was someone watching us. I thought it was Colin—I thought I saw him from the Camera Obscura.'

'Did you?' His eyes darkened swiftly. 'Why didn't you say anything?'

'Oh, that's rich!' she countered, her anger simmering over. 'I'm supposed to tell you, but you don't tell me anything! How do I know whether anything you've told me is the truth? Maybe you've been lying to me all along! Maybe Colin never stole your money—maybe you stole it yourself and put the blame on him when he found out, and now you're trying to find him so that you can shut him up for good! Damn you, let go of me!' she protested as he drew her back into his arms. 'I'll scream—even if it is only your damned spook that'll hear me!'

'I sent them away fifteen minutes ago,' he told her, restraining her struggles with effortless ease. 'And as for Colin—I had a phone call from New Zealand late this afternoon. I was going to tell you about it over dinner. They've tracked down the real Colin Clarke.'

'Oh?' She blinked up at him, startled enough to stop fighting him.

'To a cemetery in a small town near Rotoroa.' His voice was low and flat as he related the information. 'He died last year—a car accident. It appears that our Colin— or whatever his name is—adopted his identity, complete with accountancy qualifications and employment record. My people have checked back with the firms that supplied the references—they confirmed that a Colin Clarke *had* worked for them, but they didn't know he was dead.'

'Oh. . .' She wasn't sure what else to say—he had

effectively taken the wind out of her sails. 'Well, I. . .I suppose that's. . .pretty conclusive, really, then, isn't it?' she conceded wryly.

'It certainly looks that way.'

And in truth, in spite of her outburst, she had already accepted that there could be no other explanation for what had happened than that Colin had deliberately targeted her, had preyed on her loneliness, had cruelly tricked her out of the money Luke had left to keep her and Emma in security.

But somehow even that betrayal didn't hurt nearly so much as the realisation that Saul, too, had tricked her, using her to lure Colin out of whatever hole he was hiding in. Perhaps in a way she couldn't blame him, she acknowledged, in spite of the pain that was tugging at her heart. After all, there was a great deal of money involved—her money as well as his. And maybe she shouldn't be surprised—she had known that he was ruthless.

But at least Colin had only stolen her money—Saul Rainer had stolen her heart.

It cost her a considerable effort to draw back out of his arms, her hands thrust deep into her pockets as she forced herself to focus on the more serious issues. 'So, it looks as if Colin Clarke wasn't even his real name?' she queried, her voice commendably even.

He shook his head. 'We don't know that yet. It's not an uncommon name. It's possible that that was why he spotted it and chose to use it—because it was the same as his own name, so he would already have things like a birth certificate, a driving licence, a passport. All completely authentic and legal.'

'Don't the police have anything on him?'

'It doesn't look like it, although it's pretty clear he

must have done this kind of thing before. Of course, he won't have a criminal record if he's never been caught. But I've got my people onto it—they're searching through every newspaper report of similar cases in the past ten years, to see if they can track his past activities. There has to be something that will give us a clue that will lead us to him—he can't have been so clever that he's never given anything away.'

She nodded slowly, not resisting as he drew her back into the circle of his arms. She had said nothing, but the thought had been there in the back of her mind since this whole thing had begun that if Colin had been using a false name, their marriage would not have been legal. But that had probably been a little too optimistic, she conceded wryly—there was going to be no easy way out of this mess.

'What I can't understand is why he's still here when he knows we're on his trail,' she mused. 'Why take such a risk? And why put that note under my door? What could he possibly have hoped to gain by seeing me?'

'I don't know. Time, maybe? Or to find out from you how much we know?'

'I wouldn't have told him anything!' she protested, her eyes sparking in fine indignation.

He shook his head, holding her close as she tried to pull away from him. 'No. No, I don't really think you would.' He was smiling down at her in that special way that always set her pulses racing. 'I'm sorry—I should have trusted you. My instincts have been telling me from the beginning that you were straight, and they're not usually wrong.'

That dark, mesmerising gaze was holding hers, drawing her into the web of magic he could weave so easily around her. Her only defence was to close her eyes, letting her cheek rest against the hard wall of his chest. It was a little ironic that he should say he trusted her, she mused sadly, when she was still so unsure that she could trust him. Once, she would have had absolute faith in her own judgement, but now, having made such a disastrous mistake in marrying Colin, how could she ever be sure of anyone again?

'You said once that you married him because you were in love with him,' Saul remarked, an odd inflection in his voice. 'Was that really true?'

'No,' she admitted with some difficulty. 'Not really. I. . .liked him—at least, I liked the person I thought he was. But. . .I suppose I was just lonely. And somehow it seemed worse, with Christmas coming. I wasn't going to do very much, but all the shops were full of it— decorations, and presents, and Father Christmas. You couldn't get away from it. And it wouldn't have been fair on Emma not to have a proper Christmas. So in the end I went out and bought a tree—just the week before Christmas. I was trying to get off the bus with it, and he helped me. He seemed so nice, and he carried the tree all the way home, and helped me put it up, so I invited him to stay for tea, and it. . .just sort of went on from there. It was nice to have someone around, to have the company. I suppose that's not really a very good reason for getting married,' she finished lamely.

'People marry for worse reasons.'

'I suppose so. . .' She had lifted her eyes again to his, unafraid that he might read her soul, no longer able to deny the truth. 'I thought he'd make a good husband— kind, reliable. . .I wasn't really expecting anything more than that. After Luke died, I thought it wasn't worth looking for—I'd had it once, and I didn't think I could be lucky enough to find it again.'

Or could I. . .? a small voice whispered inside her head.

'It must have been something very special,' he murmured.

'Yes, it was. . .'

But, like a river flowing, life had taken her on, leaving Luke behind, as a memory—though one she would always hold close in her heart. And Luke would want her to find a love like that again. But could it be with Saul Rainer? Oh, there was no doubting the physical attraction between them—but a physical attraction could burn itself out as rapidly as it ignited. She needed something more. . .

'So what will you do now?' Saul enquired. 'You'll be getting a divorce as soon as you can?'

She sighed in wry acknowledgement. 'I suppose so. I hadn't really given it much thought.'

'You can't be expected to stay married to him,' he protested fiercely. 'Not after what he's done.'

'I know,' she conceded. 'It's just. . .somehow I hate the thought of a divorce. I suppose I'm just old-fashioned, but. . .marriage is very important to me—maybe because I was married to Luke for so long. I suppose it's silly, really. . .'

'No, it isn't silly,' he countered, his hand stroking down over her hair in a gesture of which he seemed almost unaware. 'I wonder if he'll ever realise what a fool he was?'

Shelley let her forehead rest against his chest again. This conversation was beginning to slide into dangerous territory. It could be very tempting to let herself believe that he could fall in love with her, but she wasn't sure if his idea of love was quite the same as her own. Falling in love, for her, was something serious, something that

went very deep. For him. . .well, from what she knew of
him, it was just a game.

OK, maybe the picture the tabloids painted of him
wasn't entirely accurate; in fact, she knew it wasn't—
there was much, much more to him than the shallow,
profit-grabbing womaniser they portrayed. But it would
be unrealistic to imagine that she could be the one to
persuade him of the advantages of a lifelong, one-to-one
commitment, when so many others had failed. And she
couldn't risk settling for anything less.

But his hand stroking her hair was beguiling her
senses, reminding her of that wicked temptation that was
so hard to fight. 'I want to make love to you tonight,'
he murmured, his voice low and husky. His breath was
warm against her cheek as he dusted hot kisses across
her face. 'I've never wanted anything so much in my
whole life.'

And why not? a treacherous little voice inside her head
was whispering. Just this one precious night, to give her
something she could remember down the long, lonely
years ahead. One night of perfect bliss. . . But the
memory would be tainted, her conscience reminded her
coldly. With one ugly little word—adultery—that could
never be expunged.

Dammit, why did it have to matter? Colin hadn't meant
his marriage vows—he had been lying through his teeth,
intending all the time to steal her money and run. But it
made no difference—the vows had been spoken, and
they couldn't be taken back.

With an effort of will that took every ounce of strength
she possessed, she drew back from him, shaking her
head. 'I. . .can't,' she insisted in a ragged whisper. 'At
least. . .not yet. . .'

'Then when?' he demanded forcefully.

'When I. . .when my divorce comes through.'

'But that could take months!'

'I know.'

'So, what are you going to do in the meantime?' he grated. 'Are you going to go on holding me at arm's length?'

'I'm not exactly holding you at arm's length at the moment,' she pointed out with a trembling laugh.

'Dammit, you know what I mean!' he growled, his arms tightening around her, crushing her against the hard length of his body. 'This isn't enough—I want you in my bed, I want to make love to you. I want to see you naked, I want to caress every inch of you, to kiss you until you can't breathe. . .'

Shelley drew in a sharp breath, putting her hands up between them as she tried to draw back from him. 'No. . . Saul, please,' she pleaded brokenly.

'Why not? Damn you, why not?'

'Because I'm still married!' She had to pause to draw in another deep, shuddering breath. 'I know it's stupid, but I can't help it—that's just the way I am. I just can't do it—it. . .wouldn't feel right.'

Those dark eyes were on fire, as if he was trying to use their mesmeric power to impose his will on hers. But slowly he seemed to realise that she wasn't going to change her mind, and with a low groan, almost of pain, he drew her back against him.

'All right,' he conceded rawly. 'If that's the way you want it. But just promise me one thing—that when it's all settled we can pick this thing up again from here. You know it's not going to just go away—it's much too big for that.'

His mouth came down to capture hers again in a kiss that seemed to melt something inside her. She was in love with him; it didn't seem to matter how stupid it was—it was something far beyond the reach of reason.

He wrapped the folds of his own thick woollen over-coat around them both, kissing her with an intensity that blotted out every other thought from her brain. Time swirled around them with the night mist, but she didn't want to move—she wanted to stay here for ever, wrapped up in his arms until the stars themselves grew old.

But time couldn't be denied—it was getting very late, and even the warmth of his body couldn't entirely compensate for the chilling damp that seemed to find its way inside even the double layer of coats. At long last he lifted his head, smiling down at her a little crookedly.

'We'd better be getting back to the hotel,' he murmured.

'Yes. . .'

'Do you want to take a taxi, or shall we walk?'

She slanted him a wry smile. 'I doubt if we'll get a taxi—there's hardly been any traffic along this road for the past half-hour or more. We might as well walk—it isn't too far.'

He nodded, slipping his arm loosely around her shoulders as they strolled back up the hill towards the floodlit castle, which floated like a fantasy in the mist. It was like walking in a dream—they could have been the only people in the city, in the whole world. . .

But that was all it was, she reminded herself with bitter honesty—a dream. Oh, she would go on loving him, but he. . . Though he might genuinely believe at the moment that whatever he felt for her would last until such time as her divorce from Colin set her free, she strongly doubted it. He was a very busy man—his work would quickly distract his mind. And there were plenty of other women—beautiful women—who would be more than willing to offer him consolation—women who wouldn't have the problem of finding a babysitter if he invited them out to dinner, who wouldn't walk around with an unnoticed smear of porridge on their collar, or a wax crayon melting in their pocket.

No, she was going to have to face the truth. If she didn't go to bed with him tonight—and she couldn't—she probably never would. As he had said, her divorce could take months, and by that time he would almost certainly have forgotten she even existed.

CHAPTER EIGHT

'WHY are we wasting time sitting around here?' Shelley turned from the window of the spacious sitting room in Saul's half of the suite, where she had been gazing abstractedly out of the window. It had been raining all day, sheeting down across Princes Street Gardens, and the dismal grey clouds were low enough to obscure the battlements of the castle.

Saul glanced up from the writing-desk, where he was reading through a stack of papers, between taking calls from Paris, New York, Budapest and Bangkok. 'Bored?' he teased gently.

'Yes, I am.' Feeling as edgy as a caged tiger, she paced around the room, finally plumping down in one of the comfortable armchairs arranged around a low coffee-table of gleaming, brass-bound mahogany. 'I want to get this business sorted out and go home. I. . .miss Emma.'

Which was quite true, although she was guiltily aware that it wasn't the only reason—or even, perhaps, the main reason—why she wanted to get away from Edinburgh. Last night, tossing wakefully in the wide bed in her own room, she had measured out the distance between her door and his. . . She didn't think she could take another night of that sort of temptation.

Those dark eyes glinted in mocking query. 'What do you suggest we do?'

'I don't know! You're the expert strategist,' she threw back at him irritably. 'While we're sitting here twiddling our thumbs, Colin could be getting away—he'll probably be out of the country by now.'

'I don't think so,' Saul responded with easy confidence. 'If he was going to do that, he'd have gone as soon as we arrived in Edinburgh, not spent yesterday following us around. I think he still believes he has plenty of time.' He glanced at his watch. 'Why don't you ring down to Room Service and ask them to bring us up afternoon tea—?'

'I don't want tea. . .'

A discreet tap on the door interrupted her. Saul smiled drily. 'Well, perhaps you could just see who that is, instead.'

She shot him a fulminating glare, and stalked over to snatch open the door. A young woman, wearing the smart blue suit of the hotel's staff, stood in the passage, a large white envelope bearing the hotel's blue logo in her hand.

'Mr Rainer?' she queried with a bright, professional smile. 'An urgent fax has just arrived for you.'

'Er. . .thank you.' Shelley took the envelope, and closed the door.

Saul took it from her, slitting open the end with a slim silver paper-knife. Inside were several folded sheets of slippery fax-paper, fresh from the machine and still inclined to curl themselves up awkwardly as he tried to read them.

'Is it about Colin?' Shelley demanded, unable to contain her patience as he read slowly through the sheets.

He nodded, handing her the papers. She laid them on the coffee-table, smoothing them out so that she could read the blurred print. The first one was just a standard top sheet from the firm of private investigators Saul had employed. The others were a jumble of newspaper clippings and extracts from other reports.

'They've been searching through the archives of every national and local newspaper in the country, going back ten years, looking for reports of any similar cases,' he summarised for her. 'They've finally come up with a character of about the right age and physical description. He's been involved in a whole string of similar incidents, but he's never been convicted. His most recent victim was about a year ago—a young widow in Leicester whom he cheated out of a substantial insurance pay-out on her husband's life. He's used a variety of aliases— but Colin Clarke is his real name. And he lives right here in Edinburgh.'

'Oh. . .' Shelley frowned over a photofit that had been put together a couple of years ago, during the enquiries into a previous case. It was as oddly jumbled as any photofit, and the hair was cut differently, but the resemblance was unmistakable—it was Colin. He seemed to specialise in vulnerable women, she mused, turning over the pages—and often women who had been recently bereaved, setting out to win their trust before disappearing with large sums of their money.

But this time he had made a mistake, she reminded herself grimly—in his foolish over-confidence he had broken with his usual *modus operandi*, seeking to add computer fraud to his repertoire. But in picking on Saul Rainer he had guaranteed his own destruction.

From beneath her lashes she glanced up at the man opposite her. She had known from the first time she had met him that he was ruthless—he certainly wasn't a man to let anyone cheat him. It must be costing him a great deal of money to hire this firm of private investigators— and it would have taken a colossal number of man-hours to comb through all those archives to compile this dossier. Even the police wouldn't have had the resources to do that.

She picked up the sheet with the photofit again to stare at it in puzzled bewilderment. It was a pleasant sort of face, but nothing remarkable—not the sort of person you would particularly remember. And certainly not one you would suspect of being a cold-hearted, calculating conman.

Why had she married him? How *could* she have made such a colossal misjudgement? Because like his other victims she had been lonely, vulnerable, she acknowledged wryly—not the best frame of mind in which to make a critical life decision. Which was a point worth remembering; she couldn't ever risk making another mistake like that.

With a small sigh she put the papers down. 'So—what do we do now?' she enquired.

'Now we leave it to the police,' Saul responded, folding the papers together. 'All this information has been passed on to them already. With a bit of luck, they'll be able to arrest him tonight—tomorrow at the latest.'

'If he's still in Edinburgh.' Why had he taken the risk of staying, when he must have known the net was closing? What could possibly be keeping him here? What. . .or who?

The hotel's main restaurant spared no detail of elegant luxury. Echoing the style of a painting of Madame de Pompadour, the celebrated mistress of King Louis XV, which hung in the foyer, it was decorated in soft shades of lavender, moss and rose, with delicately painted frescoed panels on the walls and ceiling, warm lighting, and masses of fresh flowers in vases all round the room, lending their subtle perfume to the air.

And theirs was certainly the best table, Shelley acknowledged wryly; set in its own embrasure beside one of the wide arched windows, its view of the castle was unsurpassed. If anything had been needed to remind her just how vast was the gulf that separated her from Saul Rainer, this would have been it.

He seemed perfectly at home here—the head waiter knew him by name, knew his preference in wines, and a message had been sent out from the head chef, no less, to enquire whether Monsieur Rainer would care for his favourite monkfish in ginger sauce, although it wasn't on the menu this evening.

Watching him across the table as he cleared his plate with relish, she was conscious of a lingering ache in the region of her heart. The flickering flame of the single tall candle in the centre of the table between them cast softening shadows across his arrogant features, and reflected like fires in the darkness of his eyes as he smiled at her.

'What's wrong? Don't you like it?' he queried, noticing that she had barely touched her own dinner.

'Oh. . . Yes, it's. . .very nice,' she managed, her voice a little unsteady. 'I just. . .I suppose I'm not very hungry, that's all.'

'Why is that?' he murmured, softly taunting, knowing full well what was responsible for taking away her appetite.

She hoped the subdued lighting would hide the blush of pink that crept up over her cheeks. 'I was just thinking about Emma,' she responded, reaching for her wineglass. 'This is the first time I've left her since she was born.'

'She'll be all right with your family.'

'I know.' She forced a laugh. 'She'll be having the time of her life, I expect, with all of them spoiling her.'

He reached across the table, and brushed his fingers across hers. 'So don't worry about her,' he coaxed softly.

'I know. I just. . .I can't help it.' She smiled at him a little crookedly. 'Maternal obsession, I suppose.' Which was as clear a message as she could convey that Emma could not, and would not, be forgotten—she would always be her first priority.

She withdrew her hand, and picked up her glass to sip the cool, dry Burgundy wine. She hadn't dared ask for a beer in here, accepting instead Saul's choice of a 'seventy-nine Montrachet' and trying not even to think of how much it cost. It had been something of a revelation—the only wine she had drunk before had been cheap supermarket plonk, mostly just at Christmas, and she had never thought much of it. But this was quite beautiful—a rich honey-yellow colour, and with a delicate, slightly fruity scent, and a flavour that lingered on the tongue, intriguingly complex. A little like the man opposite her, she mused fancifully—and very much a taste she could acquire if she allowed herself to do so.

The waiter came to clear away the plates. 'Would *madame* care to choose something from the sweet trolley?' he enquired politely.

'*Madame* will probably devour the entire contents of the sweet trolley,' Saul teased, his eyes laughing at her.

'No, I won't!' she protested, feigning indignation. 'Just one. But. . .shall I have the profiteroles, or the gateau? Or that flan looks nice—what's in it?'

'Chocolate and chestnuts, *madame*,' the waiter informed her, a twinkle in his eyes.

'Mmm—sounds gorgeous. But I think I'll have the tiramisu.' Oh, it was difficult to make a choice from the sumptuous display. 'Or maybe. . .the pavlova? No, the tiramisu,' she decided with a firm little nod. 'And coffee.'

'I'll just have coffee,' Saul added, sharing out the last of the wine in the bottle between their glasses. 'You do like your sweets, don't you?'

Shelley laughed a little unsteadily, aware that the wine—or something—was making her feel a little light-headed. 'I can resist almost anything except temptation,' she quipped, hoping a touch of humour, however corny, would convey an impression of sophisticated sang-froid—though she was rather afraid that the effect was quite the opposite.

Saul laughed softly—a husky sound that seemed to caress her. 'Is that so?' he murmured, his hard mouth curving into a slow, sensuous smile. 'I shall have to remember that.'

She felt a rush of melting warmth flood through her veins, and turned her eyes quickly away from his, reaching out with a fumbling hand for her wineglass, just for something to hold. . .and knocked it over, gasping in shock as a stain spread across the pristine linen tablecloth.

'Don't worry,' he assured her quickly as she snatched up her napkin to dab ineffectually at the damp patch. 'The waiter will deal with it.'

'I'm sorry. . .' Damn, how could she have been so clumsy? She had never felt such a fool. . .

Suddenly their table seemed to be the centre of atten-tion. She glanced up in bewilderment as the head waiter came over and bent to whisper something to Saul. Behind him stood a thick-set man in a dark overcoat, the sprink-ling of raindrops across his shoulders sparkling like sequins in the light of the crystal chandeliers that hung from the frescoed ceiling of the restaurant; it was the peaked cap of a police inspector tucked under his arm that had everyone in the room craning to see what was going on.

Shelley knew that her cheeks had flamed a vivid shade of scarlet, and was glad to be able to hide partially behind the waiter who had come to clear up the spilled wine. The police inspector was talking quietly to Saul—she couldn't quite catch what they were saying. At least that stupid accident—and its cause—was forgotten, she mused distractedly.

Saul nodded, laying his napkin on the table beside his plate, and smiled grimly across the table at Shelley. 'I'm afraid that tiramisu will have to wait,' he informed her, an inflection of sardonic humour in his voice. 'Our assistance is required.'

'They've found Colin?' she queried, wide-eyed.

'They've found an address. They need us to identify him when they make their arrest.'

'Of course. . .' She hurriedly finished her wine, and rose to her feet. 'I'm ready.'

The house was on a newly built estate in the suburbs—one of those estates of large, detached houses with brick-paved drives and separate double garages, and Georgian-style porches that looked, to her, ridiculously out of place against modern red-brick walls. Shelley couldn't imagine why anyone who could afford a house like that would want to live in one.

The police car rolled into a cul-de-sac in convoy with three others—two more had already gone to the back of the houses to cut off any escape. They were taking no chances, Shelley mused drily to herself. Already curtains were twitching at windows as neighbours peered out into the rainy night to see what was going on.

A shadow detached itself from a hedge of half-grown Leyland cypress, that bane of suburbia, and trod quickly over to report to the inspector, who nodded and turned to Saul. 'We've been watching the place for a couple of hours, but there's been no sign of activity. There's some-one inside. . .' That much was fairly obvious, since there were lights on both upstairs and downstairs. 'But we're not sure if it's Chummy or not.'

Shelley nodded slowly, staring at the house with its frou-frou curtains and dinky front-garden rockery, trying to imagine Colin living there—but she could barely even remember now what he looked like. Would she be able to identify him?

'OK. We have a warrant—let's go and see if we can pick him up.'

The inspector led the way up the path, flanked by several of his men. Shelley watched, her throat tight; there was a strange irony in waiting beside the man she was in love with, to confront the man she had married. . .

A moment's hiatus followed the inspector's peremp-tory rap on the door, and he was about to knock again when it was opened—by a woman.

Shelley stared in shock. Of course. . .she should have guessed. This was why Colin had taken the risk of linger-ing in the city when he could have got away. Suddenly a tidal wave of anger rocked her. Either the police had the wrong house, or Colin was *living* with that woman—while she had been feeling guilty about her feelings for Saul!

She was certainly exceptionally pretty, Shelley was forced to acknowledge. Baby-blonde curls framed a face as exquisite as a china doll's, and she had the figure of a pocket Venus—and, from her navy blue mascara to her high-heeled red shoes, every art of cosmetics and fashion had been employed to enhance the effect.

Shelley couldn't hear the initial exchange between the young woman and the inspector, but she saw those blue eyes widen in astonishment, saw her step back, inviting him into the house. As he went inside he gestured to one of his sergeants and Saul and Shelley to follow.

It was like walking into a doll's house, Shelley thought, gazing round in bemused astonishment. The hall and the sitting room were deeply carpeted in a totally impractical shade of pale pink, and the three-piece suite was upholstered in a rose-flowered chintz that matched the extravagantly frilled and swathed curtains at the windows. A pink and cream Chinese silk rug lay in front of the 'real-flame' gas fire in the stone fireplace, and the rest of the furniture was reproduction antique, dotted with vases of artfully arranged silk flowers.

Just inside the door was a set of very expensive matching luggage in smart red leather, piled up and apparently waiting to be taken off at any moment. The inspector eyed it questioningly. 'You were planning a trip?'

Those gleaming blonde curls bobbed as she nodded her head. 'Yes—to Lanzarote. That's in the Canary Islands,' she added helpfully, as if the inspector might be unaware of the resort's location. Her voice was as sugar-sweet as her house, high-pitched and breathy—and instantly grating on Shelley's nerves.

The inspector exchanged a brief glance with Saul that could have been one of amusement. 'May I ask your name?' he enquired, formally polite.

'Oh—of course. I'm Traci—with an 'I'. How do you do?' She smiled, innocent as a child remembering her manners.

'Traci?'

'That's right. Of Traci's Beauty Bars,' she added with an unaffected pride. 'You've heard of them?' She glanced at Shelley, apparently assuming that she, at least, would have done so. 'I've just opened up another one, just round the corner from Jenner's. It's ever so smart. We do hairdressing, of course, and manicure, and we're going to start aromatherapy. . . But why are you looking for Colin?' she interrupted herself, it apparently dawning on her somewhat belatedly to wonder why all these policemen had come to her house with a search warrant. 'Is there something wrong?'

'We believe that he may have been involved in some fraudulent activities in London,' the inspector explained in the gentle tones of an uncle talking to a very young niece.

Those blue eyes widened with a surprise that could not be anything but genuine. 'Colin? But that's ridiculous!' she protested, indignant. 'He wouldn't need to do anything like that—he makes lots of money. He's a businessman—he just got back from Bahrain a couple of weeks ago. He was out there for three months.'

'I'm afraid he wasn't,' Shelley put in, feeling rather sorry for the younger woman, but sure it was kinder to let her know the truth at once. 'He was in London.'

The blonde turned to her, bewildered. 'Who are you?' she demanded, the little-girl voice quavering.

Shelley tried to smile to soften the blow. 'I'm his wife.'

'What. . .?' The quavering voice rose into hysterics. 'But *I'm* his wife!'

'*What?*' Shelley sat down hard on one of the chintz armchairs, her head suddenly spinning. 'But. . .'

The blonde darted over to one of the many dainty little tables dotted around the room, and snatched up a photograph in a silver frame. 'We've been married for six years,' she wailed, thrusting the picture at Shelley.

Shelley found herself staring down at the photograph she held in her shaking her hands—a photograph of Traci, a fetching confection of white net and silk roses perched on her blonde curls, signing her name with a white fountain pen in a thick register of marriages, and gazing up, misty-eyed, at her proud bridegroom. Colin.

The rain had cleared, and the sky was full of stars; a sharp frost had painted every twig and branch of the trees in Princes Street Gardens with silver-dust which sparkled in the lights that were strung through their branches. Shelley stood wrapped up in the thick towelling dressing gown provided by the hotel, her forehead against the cold window-pane, gazing out at the fairy-tale scene; its unreality seemed to match perfectly the mood in her head.

Colin had been married to that woman for six years. Six years! How on earth could he have stood that inane voice for all that time? But that wasn't the main point, she reminded herself, struggling to hold onto some shreds of sanity—the point was that he had already been married when he had married her.

It had been quite apparent that 'Traci-with-an-I' had known nothing about his activities—she had genuinely believed all the stories he had told her about running an import-export company, which had often necessitated long business trips abroad. He had phoned her regularly, pretending to be calling from the Middle East, probably faking the normal sounds of the international telephone system, but he had never written. When she had finally been forced to accept the truth, she had become hysterical, and it had taken a good hour to calm her down.

Shelley had actually begun to feel rather sorry for her—she wasn't very bright but she clearly thought the world of Colin. And he must have thought a great deal of her—enough to turn to crime to keep her in the style she revelled in, enough to take the risk of staying in the city as the net closed around him so that she wouldn't be alarmed by his sudden impulsive desire to whisk her off to Lanzarote for a surprise holiday.

And much more than he ever thought of me, she acknowledged wryly. It was ironic, in a way—while she had been trying to persuade herself that she loved him, and feeling guilty because she knew she really didn't, he had never loved her at all, not one scrap. All the time his heart had truly been with that air-brained dizz with her pink carpets and little-girl voice.

That very pretty air-brained dizz, an insidious little voice inside her head whispered nastily. Jealous, are you? Wondering what Saul really thought of her? He had hardly seemed able to take his eyes off her—Shelley had been watching him covertly from beneath her lashes the whole time they had been in that cutesy little doll's house.

After all, should she be surprised? Traci-with-an-I was the sort who appealed to men—she made it her business to be, her life's work. Girlish, feminine, with not a single thought in her head that might challenge or threaten the delicate male ego. Why shouldn't Saul Rainer be as susceptible to all that as any other man?

Except that she wouldn't have taken him for such a fool, she mused bitterly. He had seemed the type who would want something more. . . And it wasn't just her own vanity that told her that the powerful physical attraction between them had been real. It might not last, but it had been real.

And now. . . Colin had slipped the net after all. He could be anywhere—it would probably take Interpol to find him. There was no longer any point to staying on in Edinburgh, waiting for him to show up again. So tomorrow they would check out of the hotel, drive back down to London, back to their normal lives—lives that had no point of contact once this episode was over. . .

Turning her head, she stared at the door—the one that led through into the other part of the suite. Saul's part. Last night it had only been her conscience that had held her back from surrendering to the temptation she really didn't want to resist—the belief that she would have been breaking her marriage vows, committing adultery.

But now she knew that Colin had already been married; his marriage to her had been bigamous. So legally she had never been married to him at all. There was no need for a divorce, nothing to stop her taking those few steps to Saul's door—nothing but her own fear of the consequences. . .

But if she stayed here, stayed safe, there would also be consequences, she reminded herself, her heart fluttering. Would she always regret that she had missed this chance, always wonder what it would have been like? Torn, she hesitated for a long moment, scarcely breathing, feeling the tension coil in the pit of her stomach. It would be just for this one night. . .

Her feet seemed to move as if of their own volition across the soft carpet, making no sound. She opened the door into the small lobby, and stood staring at the other door. It wasn't locked—the key was on this side, and she hadn't bothered to turn it. But nevertheless she knocked, her hand trembling slightly at the enormity of what she was about to do.

There was a long silence—so long that she began to wonder if he was actually in there, or was maybe already asleep. Perhaps this hadn't been a very good idea after all. . . But just as she was about to turn away she heard a footfall on the other side of the door, and it opened slowly.

He had been in the shower. His dark hair was damp and curling around his ears, and he was wearing only a white towel, slung low around his hips. She stared at him, stared at the hard male muscles beneath the bronzed, wet-sheened skin, at the powerful width of his chest scattered with rough, dark, curling hair—hair which plunged down in a deep line across the lean plane of his stomach, disappearing beneath the towel. . .

There was a question in those dark eyes, but she couldn't speak—her mouth was dry, her heart was pounding so hard that she felt dizzy. But there was no need for her to speak. He put out his hand and took hers, drawing her into the room and closing the door behind her, and without a word wrapped her up in his arms.

His mouth came down to claim hers, warm and tender, but with a hint of restrained power—a power that she knew was going to demand everything she had to give. But she wasn't going to deny him—not tonight. Tonight was theirs—there was no longer any reason to resist the temptation that had been there from the very first moment they had met. Tomorrow. . . But tomorrow didn't exist yet, and she wasn't going to allow herself to think about it until it did.

His arms around her were strong, curving her close against the hard length of his body, and she had put up her hands to his wide shoulders, thrilling to the smooth power of those hard muscles as they moved beneath his warm skin. His tongue was plundering deep into her mouth in a flagrantly sensual exploration, swirling languorously over the sensitive membranes within, making her blood race as if in a fever.

She drew back, just enough so that she could look up into his eyes, feel this moment of surrender with all her senses. 'I want to be in your bed,' she whispered raggedly. 'I want you to see me naked, I want you to caress every inch of me, to kiss me until I can't breathe. . .'

He let go of his breath in a long, deep sigh. 'At last. . .' he rasped, his fingers tangling in her hair. 'I don't think I could have waited much longer—I've been going crazy. . .'

He dragged her head back as her lips parted again to welcome the ravaging assault of his kiss. He had curved her hard against him, so that her tender breasts were crushed against the hard wall of his chest in a fierce, glorious embrace, sweeping aside any last hint of doubt that may have been lingering in the saner recesses of her mind.

But this was no time for sanity, for questioning whether she was doing the right thing—there was only the irresistible pull of her senses as she melted beneath the insistent persuasion of his lips, yielding to the sweet invasion of his tongue as with searing intensity he sought every deep, secret corner of her mouth, hungry and demanding.

The temperature was rising as he dusted scalding kisses across the trembling pulse in her temples, the delicate shell of her ear. She could hear only the ragged drag of her own breathing, mingled with his, the racing beat of her heart, as the velvet darkness of desire wrapped around them both, excluding everything else in the world.

She felt his hand slide inside the soft towelling folds of her wrap, smoothing over her silken skin, and a low moan of pleasure escaped her lips as he found the ripe, naked curve of her breast. His touch was magical, melting her helplessly into a sensuous response, as with exquisite expertise he moulded and caressed the aching swell, his palm flattening to crush the tender bud of her nipple until it throbbed beneath the swirling abrasion, a raw focus of sensation.

There was a swift impatience in his movements as he deftly unknotted the belt that held the wrap around her, and she caught her breath on a small gasp of shock and pleasure as he lifted her against him, the rough hair across his chest rasping against her heated flesh, the delicious friction sizzling through her like sparks of fire.

She twined her arms tightly around his neck as his hands slid down the length of her spine, moulding her intimately close to give her due warning of the primitive tension of male arousal that was going to demand satisfaction. A small tremor of mingled anticipation and apprehension shivered through her. This was going to be. . .memorable.

With a swift movement he scooped her up in his arms, as if she weighed no more than a feather, and carried her through the elegant drawing room of the suite, straight into his bedroom. A single low light glowed on a table beside the bed, casting warm shadows across the walls, and the curtains were still open, giving a glimpse of the floodlit castle high on its rocky crag.

The bed was wide and covered with a wine-coloured silk spread; a high canopy of gathered fabric above it created the impression of a king's bed. He laid her down gently among the masses of silk pillows, their eyes exchanging a primitive message of desire, and a slow, sensuous smile curved that hard mouth as he gazed down at her naked body with undisguised hunger.

'You're beautiful,' he murmured huskily.

'Am I?' She had hoped so much that he would think so, but she had been a little unsure, her confidence drained by Colin's treachery.

He laughed, his dark eyes flaming with heat as they

lingered over every naked curve, as her soft skin delicately flushed with desire. 'You know you are,' he
assured her, letting his hand stroke down slowly over her
body, savouring the warm silkiness of her bare flesh.
'I've wanted you from the first moment I saw you, from
the moment I held you in my arms when we were dancing. And now I've got you—every inch of you. . .'

His hand slid back, across the smooth curve of her
stomach, and she let go of her breath in a long, shuddering sigh as with one tantalising fingertip he trailed a
path over the firm, creamy ripeness of her breasts, encir-
cling the taut pink peaks, closer and closer in a lingering
torment, as his dark eyes slanted her a look of wicked
amusement.

'Every inch of you,' he reminded her softly. 'Nothing
less will do.'

'Yes,' she whispered, not shamed by her own eager
surrender. 'Please. . .'

Her spine was curling in ecstasy as he pinched teasingly at the tender buds of her nipples, and with a low
growl he bent his head, sending a tremor of exquisite
response shimmering through her as he lapped one rawly
sensitised nub with his hot, rasping tongue, nipped at it
lightly with his hard teeth.

It was the sweetest torture, from which he allowed her
no respite, his hungry mouth moving from one breast to
the other as the pleasure washed through her like a warm,
honeyed tide. And then at last he drew one nipple into
his mouth, and she gasped as the deep, rhythmic suckling
pulsed white fire into her veins.

She closed her eyes, her head tipping back against the
pillow, her lips parted as she dragged raggedly for breath.
Some part of her mind vaguely registered that she had
been a fool to succumb to the temptation to come in

here—how could she have believed she could survive a night like this with any shreds of her sanity intact? She should have opted for caution, and kept to the safety of her own room. . .

But how could she even think of caution when he was doing things like this to her? She was melting in helpless response, able to do nothing but lie back and let the exquisite sensations ripple through her, purring softly with pleasure like a half-tamed tigress.

He lifted his head to gaze down at her again, laughing in teasing mockery as she whimpered in protest that he had stopped what he was doing. 'Wanton little red-haired witch. Is this what you wanted when you came knocking on my door? Did you want me to make love to you like this?'

'Yes. . .' How could she deny it? Hungry, she reached out to touch him, needing to run her hands over the lean, hard planes of his body, to trail her fingers through the rough, curling hair that shadowed his bronzed skin. He growled—a low, husky sound of pleasure as she trailed an exploratory path of kisses along the line of his throat and down over his wide chest, the evocative musky scent of his skin inveigling her senses with every breath, stirring some deep, primitive response inside her.

It was an elemental thing, a sizzling awareness of the kinetic potential between his raw male strength and her own slender, supple femininity. Naked in the soft glow of the bedside lamp, she knelt over him, her hair a wild tumble of russet curls around her smooth shoulders, her breasts ripe and tipped with pink as she caressed him with her hands and mouth, her stomach muscles quivering with anticipation at the surrender he would soon demand.

But she hadn't touched the towel he was still wearing,

and he laughed in teasing mockery at her blushes. 'What's wrong?' he taunted, drawing her down to the bed beside him. 'You're not shy, are you?'

She lifted her eyes to his, feeling a little foolish at having to admit that she was. What on earth was wrong with her? He knew she wasn't a virgin—she had been married, she had a child, for goodness' sake! But at this moment the past meant nothing. She was trembling as he took her hand, coaxing her gently to stroke it down over the rippled muscles of his stomach, beneath the towel. . .

She drew in a long, sharp breath, burying her face in the hollow of his wide shoulder. She had known what a man he was, but now as the proof lay thick and hard against her fingertips she felt her mouth go dry.

'So. . .?' he murmured, nuzzling against her ear. 'What are you going to do about it?'

The teasing question was a challenge—and after all, what was there to be afraid of? Tentatively she let her hand trail along the length of the hard shaft, delighted at the frisson of response that shivered through him. Emboldened by this discovery of her own power, she began to stroke him, slowly, tantalising him as he had tantalised her.

'Witch,' he growled, his hard white teeth biting lightly into the smooth, creamy curve of her shoulder.

She laughed softly, her mouth renewing the exploration of his lean, masculine body, but this time hesitating at nothing, instincts as old as Eve teaching her games to play, helping her find all the sensitive places that would draw the most interesting responses from him. And he held nothing back, enjoying every ounce of pleasure she gave him, making her feel as if she really was the witchiest, wickedest creature that had ever lived.

His skin was gleaming bronze over the power of muscle and bone, hers like creamy silk over the soft contours of her naked curves, and they laughed in sheer delight as they tussled for supremacy, Shelley glorying in her own inevitable surrender to his superior strength as he forced her back onto the bed, her body quivering beneath every caress as he made good his promise to kiss her until she couldn't breathe.

His mouth was hot on her breast, his tongue rasping over the sweetly sensitive nub of her nipple as he sucked and teased it, sparking white hot darts of pleasure through her, and his hand stroked slowly down over the smooth curve of her stomach to gently coax apart her thighs, his fingertips curling through the russet crest of curls to find the soft, moist velvet between, exploring with the most exquisite touch to find the tiny seed-pearl of pleasure hidden within its folds.

Molten gold pooled in her stomach, and she sighed softly, her thighs parting wider to invite the most intimate of caresses as his finger dipped deep inside her, hinting at the demands to come. He sought her mouth with his again in a deep, tender kiss that lingered as sweetly as wine, and then moved down, savouring every inch of her body, letting his tongue teach her of pleasures beyond all her wildest imaginings, until she was pleading in an agony of need, begging incoherently for the ultimate possession.

And at long last he moved to lie above her, holding his weight from her, his eyes dark as they smiled down into hers. 'Please. . .' she whispered, moving beneath him to offer her body to his, her spine a quivering arc as he took her with one deep, powerful thrust, wrapping her up in his arms as they both lay still for one endless, incredible moment to feel the pure, sweet intensity of this ultimate union.

And then slowly he began to move, building an easy rhythm, now shallow, now deep, now grinding in lazy circles to stretch her deliciously as her spine curled in ecstasy and she cried out on sobbing breaths, her body on fire and her heart lost in love. He was moving her to his will as she surrendered totally to his fierce demand, their sweat-slicked bodies tumbling on the wide bed, the soft glow of the lamp casting shadows on their skin.

She had never known that such a wanton, sensual creature lay inside her; she had never known that she could respond like this. Her body was burning with an unquenchable fever, a delicious tension coiling inside her, as with each plunging thrust he sent her soaring higher and higher on wings of flame, spinning in a dizzying vortex, until at long last she heard her own voice in a strange, strangled cry, and felt the heat explode inside her, searing her brain and melting her bones, leaving her weak and helpless, as with a last deep shudder he fell into her arms and they both collapsed, spent and exhausted, tangled up in the sheets.

CHAPTER NINE

SHELLEY woke as an early ray of sunshine, creeping past the battlements of the castle high on its rocky crag, slanted in through a gap in the curtains. Saul was still asleep, his face half buried in the pillow, one arm casually thrown across her body in a gesture she would have liked to think of as possessive.

She lay for a while, watching as he slept, listening to the sound of his breathing, deep and even, consciously seeking to absorb every detail about him to add to the store of memories she could keep and treasure in the lonely times that lay ahead—the way his long, silken lashes cast faint shadows across his cheekbones, the way his dark hair curled at the nape of his neck, the way the soft morning light sculpted the hard ridges of muscle down his back.

'I love you,' she mouthed, soundlessly so that he wouldn't hear, her heart aching. If only. . .

Slipping out of bed, she reached for her towelling wrap, which had somehow ended up on the far side of the room, and, knotting the tie belt around her slim waist, she padded quietly over to the window.

Even in the cool, clear light of morning the castle looked like something out of a fairy tale, conjuring in her vivid imagination scenes of knights and ladies in fine costumes, riding out on prancing horses to watch a tournament on the green swathe of the gardens below. And last night she had been a princess in her own fairy tale, she mused wistfully, turning to gaze at Saul again, her body still warm with the memory of the way he had made love to her, again and again through the night.

It had been incredible, like nothing she would ever have imagined. And she could never have believed that she could respond like that. She had been happy with Luke; he had been like a great cuddly teddy bear, always gentle. With Colin. . . Well, perhaps it would be better to draw a veil over that. But Saul had awoken something in her that she had never known existed.

But fairy tales had no place in the real world, she reminded herself firmly—she had responsibilities. Emma. She didn't want her to become one of those confused little waifs, bewildered by a succession of men through her mother's life. She had believed that in Colin she had found a man willing to make a lasting commitment, but it had turned out to be a disaster. She wasn't going to take any more risks. She might have fallen foolishly in love with Saul Rainer, but she would throw that love away rather than let her daughter suffer a single moment's unhappiness.

Saul stirred and sat up, yawning and stretching his arms above his head to ease the muscles in his wide shoulders. His dark eyes glinted with wicked intent as he smiled at her. 'You're up early this morning.'

She shrugged in casual unconcern, trying hard to hide the effect of that smile. 'Not really—I'm usually up before seven,' she responded lightly.

'Come back to bed,' he coaxed, his voice taking on a huskier timbre.

'Why?'

He laughed softly, teasingly. 'You have a very short memory. Because I want to make love to you again, of course.'

Her body, treacherously undermining her will, was

already beginning to respond. But she shook her head, struggling to hold onto the resolution she had just made. 'No. I. . .can't.'

'Why not?' he demanded, a swift frown darkening his brow. 'Surely you don't feel guilty about last night? You've done absolutely nothing wrong—you were never legally married to that hell's spawn in the first place.'

'I know—it isn't anything to do with that.' She had to draw in a long, steadying breath, forcing herself to say what she had to say. 'It's just. . .I'm not going to have an affair with you.'

'Oh?' He arched one dark eyebrow in sardonic enquiry. 'What makes you think I was asking you to?'

His words slashed into her heart like a knife, and she had to turn quickly back to the window, struggling to blink back the tears that were stinging her eyes. It hadn't occurred to her that he had intended it to be just a one-night stand. But she couldn't pretend that he had lied to her—he had never implied that he was offering anything more. 'I'm. . .sorry,' she whispered, shame tingeing her cheeks a deep shade of scarlet. 'I suppose that was a little presumptuous of me. . .'

He slid out of bed and crossed the room in two strides, taking her firmly in his arms, refusing to allow her to resist. 'You crazy little fool,' he chuckled, dropping a kiss on the top of her lowered head. 'I don't want an affair with you—I want to marry you.'

Startled, she blinked up at him, the expression in those deep dark eyes making her heart skid and race out of control. 'Marry me? But. . .I didn't think. . . You never said. . .'

He smiled down at her in wry self-mockery. 'That I love you? I admit it took me a while to figure out that was what it was—I'd never felt like it before, and I wasn't sure I liked it in the beginning. But I think I fell in love with you before I even met you—when I saw that photograph on Colin's desk, of this kooky-looking woman with wild red hair and unbelievable earrings. And the most kissable mouth I ever saw,' he added, his own coming down to claim its sweetness.

What could she do? Her lips parted hungrily to welcome him, her arms wrapping around his shoulders as she curved herself against him, surrendering to the temptation she knew she couldn't fight. His tongue was sweeping deeply into her mouth, swirling over the sensitive membranes within, igniting the still glowing embers of desire.

They had made love all night, tumbling on the wide bed like two wild animals, caught up in the primeval spell of passion. But it had done nothing to abate the fierce need inside her—on the contrary, it had fuelled it, until it was ready to explode into a new conflagration at the slightest touch.

And as he lifted her in his strong arms and carried her back to the bed she felt the need rise again, and wrapped her arms around his neck, drawing him down to her, her hands caressing his lean, hard body as he caressed hers, and they both drowned in kisses that lingered for a thousand years.

They had breakfast in bed, feeding each other smoked salmon on scrambled egg. Shelley let herself enjoy it, but the reservations still lingered in her mind. It would be so easy, so treacherously easy, to believe that everything would work out—or was that just the triumph of hope over experience?

It was almost ten o'clock before they finally got up. Shelley went through to her own room to dress. She was just fastening her earrings into her ears—a fairly moderate pair strung with brown glass beads—when Saul came into the room, coming over to wrap his arms around her from behind and bend his head into the hollow of her shoulder, his hot tongue tracing tiny circles over the sensitive pulse point there.

'Mmm—your skin tastes delicious,' he murmured. 'Let's go back to bed.'

She laughed a little unsteadily, easing away from him. 'No, I have to give Eileen a ring and let her know what time we'll be back to pick Emma up.'

'OK,' he conceded with a wry smile. He stood back a little, his hands thrust casually into the pockets of his trousers, watching her as she fussed unnecessarily with her earrings and her hair. 'You haven't actually given me an answer yet, you know.'

'I know.' The pain inside her was like a lead weight, dragging on her heart. 'There were two photographs on Colin's desk,' she reminded him tentatively. 'The other one was Emma.'

'I know that.' His dark brows drew together in a sharp frown. 'What were you thinking? That I wouldn't want her with us? Of course I do.'

'I thought you didn't like children?' she challenged, her eyes meeting his in the mirror.

He shook his head, a twist of impatience in the hard line of his mouth. 'I never said that. I'm just not used to them, that's all. Give me time.'

He moved to take her in his arms again, but she stepped quickly away, turning towards him. 'I. . .can't,' she insisted, the conflict inside her tearing her apart. 'If this doesn't work out between us. . .it wouldn't be fair on her. She'd just be getting used to you. I made a mistake with Colin—how can I know it wouldn't happen again?'

'I'm not Colin,' he reminded her on a note of asperity. He caught her hand, drawing her inexorably towards him. 'Trust me. This will work out.'

It took every ounce of will-power she possessed to resist her own deep longing to surrender, to agree to whatever he wanted. But she knew what she had to do—she mustn't allow him to change her mind. 'You can't guarantee that. . .' she persisted, her voice faltering. 'No one can. And I'm not going to let Emma be the type of child who grows up with a series of stepfathers—I wouldn't do that to her.'

Those dark eyes gazed down into her face, as if searching right into her soul. 'So what are you saying?' he queried softly. 'You won't have an affair with me, you won't marry me—ever? Last night was all we're ever going to have?'

'Yes.' She had to turn away, unable to bear being so close to him. 'I'm sorry.'

'I see.' He moved across the room and sat down, his expression dark and unreadable. Shelley watched him, waiting, wondering what he was thinking—wishing it didn't have to be this way. But he was strong; if she had done any real damage to his heart, it would heal, and he would forget her. She wasn't so sure that her own could be so easily repaired.

'I'll. . .ring Eileen, and then we can get going—if you're ready,' she suggested awkwardly.

The telephone was on the table beside the bed. She sat down, picking up the receiver and dialling the number. It rang a few times, and then she heard her stepmother's voice saying hello. With an effort of will, she made her voice sound bright, happy—emotions she wasn't sure she would ever feel again.

'Eileen? It's me—Shelley.'

'Oh, hello, dear. How are you? Thank you for calling. Did you have a good trip? Emma was as good as gold—we absolutely loved having her. But I'm so glad everything has worked out with you and Colin after all—I knew it must have all been a silly misunderstanding. You're lucky to have such a nice husband—'

'Pardon?' Shelley interrupted the flow, startled. 'What are you talking about?'

'You and Colin, dear.' Eileen laughed indulgently. 'He told me all about it. But these things happen in the best of marriages, you know—sometimes you have to make adjustments on both sides.'

Shelley frowned at the receiver. 'You mean Colin's been there? To your house?' she queried sharply.

'Of course he has, dear,' Eileen responded, sounding vaguely puzzled. 'He came to pick up Emma—'

'He *what*?'

'He came to pick up Emma. About an hour ago. To take her home. I. . .thought they must be with you by now.' A note of uncertainty had crept into her stepmother's voice. 'Is there. . .something wrong?'

'He's taken Emma?' Shelley felt a tide of panic rise to her throat. Instinctively she turned to Saul, who had come at once to her side.

He took the phone from her, and she heard him checking the details of what had happened with Eileen. 'OK—thank you. No, don't worry—we'll find her,' he asserted grimly. 'She won't come to any harm. Shelley will ring you as soon as we catch up with them. Goodbye, Eileen.'

He put the phone down slowly, and than squatted on his haunches in front of Shelley, taking both her hands firmly in his. 'He won't hurt her,' he promised, his eyes holding hers, his voice conveying a conviction she needed desperately to cling to. 'We'll get her back safely.'

'But why has he taken her?' she asked, too numb with shock even to shed a tear.

'It's his last throw of the dice,' he surmised grimly. 'He's probably planning to hold her hostage, to try to force us to drop all the charges against him.'

'Anything,' she whispered quaveringly. 'I'll do anything.' A sharp stab of guilt knifed into her. If she had rung Eileen two hours ago, if she hadn't let herself be lured back into Saul's arms, into his bed. . . 'We have to find her.' She began to shake. 'If anything happens to her. . .'

He shook his head. 'She'll be all right,' he assured her again, wrapping his arms around her comfortingly. 'Come on, let's get going.'

'But where do we start looking?' she protested, letting him draw her to her feet.

'With Traci. If she has any brain cells in that pretty blonde head, she may be able to give us some clue as to where he could be.'

'You don't think she'll have gone with him?' Shelley queried in agitation as they drove onto the estate where Colin had lived.

Saul shook his head. 'She's dim, but she's honest,' he assured her. 'I just hope she can give us some idea where he might have bolted to.'

All the curtains in the house were still closed. At least that seemed to indicate that there was someone still at home, Shelley mused, trying to find some small shred of hope to hold onto. They parked the car on the drive and walked up to the front door. Saul rang the bell, and it pealed a melodic tune somewhere in the house.

There was a pause, and then a small voice called, 'Just a minute.'

It was actually several minutes before the door opened. Traci was wearing a very fetching wrap of palest pink silk chiffon, trimmed with marabou, but though she had bravely tried to disguise the evidence with make-up her pretty face was ravaged by tears. She looked a little surprised to see them, but held the door open to let them into the house, casting an anxious glance around the cul-de-sac to see whether any of the neighbours were watching.

'Won't you sit down?' she invited with conscientious politeness, showing them into the sitting room. 'Can I get you a cup of coffee or anything?'

'No, thank you,' Saul responded, a careful restraint in his voice so as not to alarm her. 'Traci, I know you said last night you had no idea where Colin is, but could you think again? Is there *anywhere* he might have gone?'

She shook her head, her smooth brow furrowed in concentration beneath that fluff of blonde curls. 'I honestly don't know where he is,' she sighed. 'I'd tell you if I did; I really would. I was supposed to get a taxi to the airport last night and meet him there, but the police told me he didn't show up.'

'Please,' Shelley persisted urgently. 'Try to think. He's taken my daughter—she's not even two years old yet.'

Traci's saucer-shaped blue eyes widened in genuine sympathy. 'Oh, dear! Oh, my goodness, you poor thing! Oh, I wish I could help, I really do. . .'

'Does he have any relatives anywhere? Friends?'

Traci shook her head again, nibbling on the corner of her lips in the effort of thought.

'Has he ever mentioned anywhere he particularly

likes? Anywhere he might want to go for a holiday? Anywhere he would go if he was in difficulties?'

A light slowly dawned, as Shelley struggled to control the urge to shake the information out of the girl. 'He once said Ireland was a good place to go,' she said. 'We were watching a programme on the telly about this man who had been in a gang who'd done a robbery, only it had all gone wrong and some of the gang had been arrested, and the others had blamed him and so he was on the run from the police as well as from the other robbers. . . Anyway, Colin said he should go to Ireland— he said you wouldn't have any trouble getting there because you didn't need a passport.'

Saul and Shelley exchanged glances. It was a crumb. . . '*Where* in Ireland?' Shelley demanded, her patience wearing ragged.

Traci shrugged her slender shoulders in the pretty peignoir. 'I don't know—just Ireland,' she responded vacuously. 'Is that any help?'

'Yes,' Saul responded firmly, forestalling Shelley's sharp expletive. 'Thank you, Traci.' He rose to his feet, putting a hand beneath Shelley's elbow to compel her to do the same. 'I'm sorry we can't stay—we have to hurry if we're going to catch up with him. Goodbye. It was nice to have met you again.'

'Oh, and you—of course,' Traci responded, her smile appearing briefly like the sun between the clouds. 'I do hope you find your daughter.'

'Thank you,' Shelley said weakly, and allowed herself to be hustled out to the car. 'Ireland!' she wailed as Saul started up the engine and pulled smartly off Traci's expensive brick-paved drive. 'How on earth are we going to find him there?'

'Hopefully, we'll find him before he gets there,' Saul

responded grimly. 'I doubt if he'll fly—it'd be too much
hassle with the baby, and he'd risk being noticed.
Besides, he'll want his car when he gets to the other side.
So he'll take the ferry—either Fishguard or Holyhead.
And I'll take a bet it's Holyhead—it's little further, but
it's busier and easier to get to.'

'But it's much nearer to London than here,' she
objected. 'And he's already got almost two hours'
start on us.'

'I know.' That hard mouth had curved into a smile
that held a dangerous hint of menace. 'But we're going
to fly there.'

This took more than just money, Shelley reflected as the
small plane circled over the green fields of Anglesey and
came in to land—although money had been useful. But
this took clout. Saul had simply made a call on his car
phone, and when they had arrived at Edinburgh airport
the plane had been waiting for them, ready fuelled and
with the flight-plan filed. And now they were about to
land at an RAF station. That wasn't the sort of thing just
anyone could get permission for.

And when they landed there was a car waiting for
them to drive on the ten or so miles to the ferry port on
the north-west tip of the island. The road was only a
narrow two lanes, often frustratingly blocked by traffic
where it was impossible to overtake, but Saul was an
excellent driver, making the most of every opportunity—
even Shelley, desperate with anxiety, couldn't complain
at the progress they made.

At last they reached the town, where signposts pointed
the way to follow through the streets, until she could
actually see one of the big white boats at its dock, its
huge doors open ready to load its cargo of vehicles.

'Hurry!' she pleaded, leaning forward and gripping the dashboard.

Saul smiled grimly, nodding towards the traffic light that was still on red. 'We'll be there in a moment,' he assured her in that tone of calm authority that always managed to convince her that he could sort out any problem that existed. But could he sort this one?

The lights changed, and the line of traffic rolled forward, streaming round towards the ferry terminal. Ahead Shelley could see the vehicle checkpoint, and beyond it the cars queuing in the car park, waiting to board the ferry. Was Colin there? It wouldn't be easy to spot one nondescript pale blue saloon among all those cars.

The line of traffic had come to a halt again as the checkpoint controllers in their fluorescent yellow waistcoats checked tickets and directed drivers into the appropriate lane. Too impatient to wait, Shelley unfastened her seat belt and scrambled out. 'Park there!' she shouted to Saul, pointing to a small lay-by at the side of the road, where tourists who weren't actually going on the ferry could look out over the cold Irish Sea.

A crisp wind was blowing but she didn't even notice; all her attention was on those lines of cars. Behind her she heard footsteps as Saul caught up with her. Pale blue. . .pale blue. . . Or could he have cheated them by trading in his old car for a different one, maybe even hiring one?

'There it is!' She knew it by the faded striped cushion on the rear shelf. And she could just see the top of the dark blue patterned car seat. Colin must have spotted her at the same moment, and pulled out sharply from the queue he had been waiting in, into an empty lane beside it. 'Stop him!' she shrieked at the top of her voice as he accelerated towards the exit road.

Saul ran, catching at the handle of the passenger door and wrenching it open. Trying to shake him off, Colin braked sharply, and slammed into reverse, hitting another car. As Shelley screamed, the passenger door slammed into Saul, but he wrenched at it, pulling it half off its hinges. And then, as the gears grated again, he scrambled round to the front of the car to prevent Colin from driving off.

Except he did. Staring in open-mouthed horror, Shelley saw Saul thrown onto the bonnet of the car as it accelerated away again. It was carrying him along as it lurched towards the exit from the car park; he seemed to be clinging on somehow, which meant that Colin couldn't see through the windscreen. . . The car smashed into the ticket booth at what must have been more than twenty miles an hour, hurling Saul off the bonnet like a rag doll.

'Saul!' Shelley was running, screaming in panic and distress, torn between her lover and her daughter as she reached the wreckage. Emma's cries turned her towards the car first. The car horn was wailing as Colin slumped over the steering wheel, but she ignored him, tipping up the passenger seat to lean into the back.

Emma's small face was red, and she was waving her fists, but as she saw Shelley she reached out her arms. Relief flooding through her, Shelley snatched open the seat belt and pulled her out, hugging her close, blessing the child-seat for saving her from any injury.

But the silence of the small crowd gathered around Saul was ominous. Scarcely able to breathe for the tightness in her throat, she pushed her way through to the front. He had been lying on his back, but a young woman from one of the cars, and one of the staff from the terminal, had turned him into the recovery position.

People moved back to let her pass, and she walked slowly round to his head, still clutching Emma, who had quietened now. Kneeling beside him, she stared down at his unnaturally pale face, not even aware of the tears rolling down her cheeks. 'Saul?' she whispered unsteadily.

'He's unconscious,' the young woman explained in a soft Irish brogue. 'He took a nasty knock on the head, but he's breathing.' She smiled reassuringly. 'I'm a doctor. Are you his wife?'

The hospital room was quiet except for the sound of Saul's breathing. Shelley sat beside the bed, watching him anxiously. He was lying propped up on three pillows, his arm held up in a sling above the bed, his wide chest banded with white tape to support the three broken ribs he had sustained in the accident. It was late in the evening, but he still hadn't regained consciousness, in spite of the doctors' reassurances.

Somewhere else in the hospital Colin lay, guarded by a policeman to ensure that this time he didn't get away, but she didn't care; she hadn't even glanced in his direction as he was being loaded into the ambulance. They had given Emma the once-over in Casualty, but she had been completely unhurt, and an hour ago Eileen and her father had arrived to take care of her, so that Shelley could sit with Saul.

Had his eyelids flickered just then? She leaned forward, squeezing his hand—and he seemed to squeeze back. 'Saul?' she whispered eagerly.

A dark gleam showed beneath his lashes—such long, silky lashes, incongruously feminine against such a hard-boned, masculine face. She held her breath. . .and then he smiled. 'Hello, witch. . .'

His eyes closed as he slipped back into sleep again, but it was enough. He had recognised her—the doctors had said that was the most important thing.

The door behind her opened, and one of the nurses came in. 'Hello, Mrs Rainer,' she greeted her softly. 'How is he?'

'I think he's getting better,' Shelley responded happily. 'He opened his eyes a moment ago, and he seemed to recognise me. He said hello.'

'Ah—that's good. Mr Rainer, I'm just going to take your temperature and blood pressure,' she added in a louder voice, leaning over the bed.

There seemed to be no response, even when the nurse wrapped the binding on his arm and took his blood pressure. Shelley began to get worried again. Had she imagined that brief moment of waking? Had he relapsed again?

'That's fine,' the nurse declared as she entered the figures on the chart and collected up her equipment. 'Don't worry, Mrs Rainer; he'll be all right. The doctor said the scan shows no sign of brain injury, and he'll soon get over those broken bones—he's a very strong man, your husband,' she added, slanting him an admiring glance.

'Thank you,' Shelley murmured, resuming her post at his side and taking his hand again.

As the door closed behind the nurse, she became aware of that dark gleam beneath his lashes again, this time glinting with mocking amusement. *'Mrs Rainer?'* he repeated quizzically.

Shelley felt a vivid blush of pink rise to her cheeks— she hadn't realised that he had heard that. 'I'm. . .sorry,' she murmured. 'I told them I was your wife so they'd let me stay with you.'

He smiled—that slow, sensuous smile that made her heart tingle. 'That's OK. I won't give you away,' he promised.

She peeped at him shyly, and lowered her eyes again quickly to gaze down at their two hands, entwined on the counterpane. 'Is. . .the offer still open?' she enquired tentatively.

'Why?'

Her eyes flew anxiously to his face, but saw that he was laughing, teasing her. She felt her heart begin to soar. 'Because if it is,' she responded, the blush deepening, 'I *would* like to marry you. Please.'

'Well, well!' He feigned exaggerated surprise. 'Is this a proposal?'

'Yes, it is!' she admitted, heat flooding through her.

He chuckled, taunting her with a playful mimicry of her own, earlier reservations. 'I really don't know. How do I know I can trust you?'

'Oh, damn you!' she threw at him, laughing. 'I'm sorry I was so silly. It was just. . .I was so cracked up by what Colin did that. . .I didn't trust myself. I'd. . .fallen in love with you, and I was afraid I was letting that colour my judgement. I was afraid of making another mistake.'

His smile, once so rare, was as warm as the sun. 'I understand,' he assured her, lifting her hand to lay a row of tender kisses along her knuckles. 'But this isn't a mistake.'

'I know.' Her eyes were glowing as they gazed into his. 'It was Emma I was worrying about mostly—she needs a father who'll really care for her, someone she'll always be able to rely on. I was afraid you wouldn't want to take on that sort of commitment. But you risked your life to rescue her—she couldn't have a better father than that.'

'It's a big responsibility,' he acknowledged seriously. 'But she's a great kid—bright as a button. If she turns out half as cute as her mother, she'll be doing well. And if making her mother happy is part of the job I think I'm uniquely qualified.'

'Oh?' She arched one finely drawn eyebrow in quizzical enquiry. 'Modest, aren't you?'

'Not unnecessarily so,' he retorted, lounging back languidly against the pillows. 'Besides, you shouldn't risk arguing with me—I'm a seriously injured man.'

She glared at him, mock-fierce. 'Argue with you? If you're not careful, I'll break the rest of your ribs!'

He laughed at that—a rich, mellow sound that set her heart singing. 'That's my Shelley,' he declared, slipping his good arm around her and drawing her up onto the bed, holding her close. 'My beautiful red-haired witch—I adore you!'

MILLS & BOON®

Next Month's Romances

♡

Each month you can choose from a wide variety of romance novels from Mills & Boon. Below are the new titles to look out for next month from the Presents and Enchanted series.

Presents™

SEDUCING THE ENEMY	Emma Darcy
WILDEST DREAMS	Carole Mortimer
A TYPICAL MALE!	Sally Wentworth
SETTLING THE SCORE	Sharon Kendrick
ACCIDENTAL MISTRESS	Cathy Williams
A HUSBAND FOR THE TAKING	Amanda Browning
BOOTS IN THE BEDROOM!	Alison Kelly
A MARRIAGE IN THE MAKING	Natalie Fox

Enchanted™

THE NINETY-DAY WIFE	Emma Goldrick
COURTING TROUBLE	Patricia Wilson
TWO-PARENT FAMILY	Patricia Knoll
BRIDE FOR HIRE	Jessica Hart
REBEL WITHOUT A BRIDE	Catherine Leigh
RACHEL'S CHILD	Jennifer Taylor
TEMPORARY TEXAN	Heather Allison
THIS MAN AND THIS WOMAN	Lucy Gordon

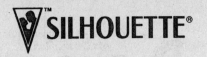

™SILHOUETTE®

Tempting…Tantalising…Terrifying!

Strangers
in the night

Three spooky love stories in one compelling
volume by three masters of the genre:

Dark Journey by Anne Stuart
Catching Dreams by Chelsea Quinn Yarbro
Beyond Twilight by Maggie Shayne

Available: July 1997   Price: £4.99

SUMMER SEARCH

How would you like to win a year's supply of Mills & Boon®
books? Well you can and they're FREE! Simply complete the
competition below and send it to us by 31st December 1997.
The first five correct entries picked after the closing date will
each win a year's subscription to the Mills & Boon series of
their choice. What could be easier?

SPADE

SUNSHINE

PICNIC

BEACHBALL

SWIMMING

SUNBATHING

CLOUDLESS

FUN

TOWEL

SAND

HOLIDAY

W	Q	T	U	H	S	P	A	D	E	M	B
E	Q	R	U	O	T	T	K	I	U	I	E
N	B	G	H	L	H	G	O	D	W	K	A
I	I	O	A	I	N	E	S	W	Q	L	C
H	N	U	D	D	F	W	P	E	O	H
S	U	N	B	A	T	H	I	N	G	L	B
N	S	E	A	Y	F	C	M	D	A	R	A
U	B	P	K	A	N	D	M	N	U	T	L
S	E	N	L	I	Y	B	I	A	N	U	L
H	B	U	C	K	E	T	N	S	N	U	E
T	A	E	W	T	O	H	G	H	O	T	F
C	L	O	U	D	L	E	S	S	P	W	N

C7F

Please turn over for details of how to enter ☞

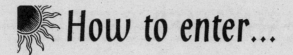

How to enter...

Hidden in the grid are eleven different summer related words. You'll find the list beside the word puzzle overleaf and they can be read backwards, forwards, up, down and diagonally. As you find each word, circle it or put a line through it. When you have found all eleven, don't forget to fill in your name and address in the space provided below and pop this page in an envelope (you don't even need a stamp) and post it today. Hurry competition ends 31st December 1997.

Mills & Boon Summer Search Competition
FREEPOST, Croydon, Surrey, CR9 3WZ
EIRE readers send competition to PO Box 4546, Dublin 24.

Please tick the series you would like to receive if you are a winner

Presents™ ❑   Enchanted™ ❑   Temptation® ❑

Medical Romance™ ❑   Historical Romance™ ❑

Are you a Reader Service™ Subscriber?   Yes ❑   No ❑

Ms/Mrs/Miss/Mr _____

(BLOCK CAPS PLEASE)

Address _____

_____

_____ Postcode _____

(I am over 18 years of age)